JIMGRIM AND THE "IBLIS" AT LUDD

JIMGRIM AND THE "IBLIS" AT LUDD

TALBOT MUNDY

WILDSIDE PRESS

Originally published in *Adventure*, January 10, 1922

Published by Wildside Press LLC.
www.wildsidebooks.com

CHAPTER I

"Lead on, Jimgrim sahib. I have seen the day when stronger boars than that one bit the dust!"

As a General rule when Major Jim Grim strode into the administrator's office in the former German hospice, now British headquarters in Jerusalem, it was to be greeted with that kind of confident familiarity that, from his official superior, warms the fiber of a man's being. Jim's standing in the administrator's favor was the cause of a good deal of jealousy; more than one British officer resented the frequent private consultations between Sir Henry Kettle and the American, although they could not prevent them.

They might have felt less jealous if they had known of the wholesale disregard of personal feelings (Jim's especially) whenever the administrator considered him at fault.

Jim walked into the administrator's private office three mornings after having run to ground the Dome of the Rock conspirators, rather expecting the usual smile and exchange of unusual jokes before broaching the day's business. But Sir Henry Kettle opened on him without formality, with blazing eyes and a voice like flint.

"Look here, Grim, what the hell do you mean by this? I've received complaint of insolence and insubordination, made against you by Brigadier-General Jenkins. It came in the morning mail from Ludd. Were you insolent to him?"

"Maybe."

"Insubordinate?"

"That'ud be a matter of opinion, sir."

"Do you realize that if he presses these charges there'll be a court martial, and you'll be broke?"

"I didn't tell him what I thought of him because he was acting like a gentleman," Jim answered.

"That isn't the point. Jenkins may be a lot of things without that excusing you in the least. What I demand to know is, how dare you risk my having to court martial you and lose your services?"

There was not any answer Jim could make to that, so he said nothing.

"Are you under the impression that because an exception was made in your case, and you were recognized as an American citizen when given a commission in the British Army, that therefore you're at liberty to ignore all precedent and be insolent to whom you please? If so, I'll disillusion you!"

Jim knew his man. He wanted none of that kind of disillusionment. He continued to hold his tongue, standing bolt upright in front of the administrator's desk.

"Apply your own standards if you like. How long would insolence from major to brigadier be tolerated in the United States Army?"

That was another of those questions that are best left alone, like dud shells and sleeping TNT.

"Jenkins writes that you gave him the lie direct. Is that true?"

"No. I asked him a question he couldn't answer without telling a lie, or else retracting what he'd said."

"He says he offered to fight him."

"Not quite. He was afraid to go to you with a lame story, and wanted me to help soak Catesby with all the blame for losing that TNT. I know Catesby—know him well. I told Jenkins that if it'ud make him like himself any better he might put the gloves on with me any time he sees fit. It was unofficial—not in front of witnesses—and it stands. He took me up; said he'd give me the thrashing of my life. He also promised not to make a goat of Catesby."

"Well, he has charged Captain Catesby with neglect of duty in permitting those two tons of TNT to be stolen from a truck on a railway siding. Catesby is under arrest."

"May I say what I think about that, just between you and me?"

"Certainly not! But for your insolence to Jenkins I could have brought him to book over this business. Do you see the predicament you've put me in? This isn't the first time Jenkins has covered his own shortcomings by putting blame on a subordinate. I've been watching my chance to turn you loose on him. He gives it to my by accusing Catesby, and you spoil it! You're the one man Jenkins is afraid of; but how can I send you to investigate him now without upholding a breach of discipline?"

"I'll do anything to make amends that you would do, sir, if you stood in my shoes," said Jim.

"I can't imagine myself in your shoes," Kettle retorted. "I was never guilty of insubordination in my life."

"Maybe you never had reason," Jim answered. "What I said to him was in private. There were no witnesses, but he promised not to make a goat of Catesby. It's his word against mine, and if he dares press that charge against me I shall call him a liar in open court, and take the consequences."

"You'll do nothing of the kind. You'll go to Ludd at once, clear Captain Catesby if you can, find the real culprit, and do your utmost to whitewash Jenkins in the process.

"I'm leaving for Ludd by motor in twenty minutes myself. I shall see Jenkins and arrange that he'll accept an apology, which you will make to him the moment you arrive. Do you understand me?"

"I understand I'm to apologize. Yes, I'll do that, since you wish it."

"Stay at Ludd until you've cleaned up," the administration added deliberately. "There has been a lot of thieving down there that looks like organized conspiracy. Dig to the bottom of it. That's all."

* * * *

Outside the room Jim lit a cigarette and chuckled to himself. If there was one man on earth whom he despised and hated it was Brigadier-General Jenkins.

Nor was he alone in that particular. He more than suspected that the administrator shared his feelings; and he knew for a fact that half the British Army in Palestine loathed the man for his blatant self-advertising.

So to be told to go to work to whitewash Jenkins appealed to his sense of humor, the more so as he divined that underneath the administrator's actual words there lay another meaning. Jim and Sir Henry Kettle understood each other pretty accurately as a rule. Discipline was to be upheld at all costs. Well and good; he would apologize. But since half-measures formed no part of Jim's philosophy, he decided to carry out the administrator's instructions to the letter and to find some way of giving Jenkins such an elegant coat of white as should embarrass even that praise-hungry brigadier.

Fair play and Sir Henry Kettle were synonymous terms. Therefore there was more in this than met the eye. Therefore— "Forward, march!"

He walked down the echoing corridor chuckling to himself, and almost ran into Colonel Goodenough, a commander of Sikhs who cherished a good soldier as he did a horse.

"Morning, Grim. Got a K.C. B. or something? What's the good news? Share it!"

"I'm off to Ludd."

"Good Ludd deliver us! Fleas—sand—centipedes—raw recruits—sick horses—thieves—and the man's happy! Are there any more at home like you?"

"I need one of your men to go with me, sir."

"So that's the joke, is it? Well, it's on you. You can't have him. I'm short of men. There seem to be only two classes of people in universal demand in Jerusalem—Sikhs and jailbirds; jailbirds for the dirty work, and Sikhs to push perambulators. Every man in my regiment has two men's work to do. I won't spare one of them."

"Lend me Narayan Singh, sir."

"Why, damn it, he's my best man!"

"Sure. That's why I want him."

"He's priceless. If you want my private opinion he could run the regiment better than I can. Why, I use that man to teach my officers their business."

"Reward him then," Jim answered. "Give him a job after his own heart. Send him with me."

"For how long?"

"Indefinite. I'm to smell out the thieves at Ludd."

"Well—it's true—that would be a picnic for Narayan Singh. He deserves a treat. But if you get him killed or seriously injured I'll murder you. Why, I spent all one night in No Man's Land at Gaza hunting for that man rather than lose him; I wouldn't have done as much for my grandmother."

"That how you got the V.C.?"

"Damn it, yes. And Narayan Singh got nothing, although I recommended him until I was sick of writing letters. He'd done ten time what I did. If you borrow him, I want him back all in one piece marked 'perishable.' Watch that he doesn't get malaria down at Ludd. Don't overwork him. See that he gets regular meals. I tell you, that man's precious!"

"How soon can I have him?"

"I'm on my way to the lines now. Come in my car and get him."

* * * *

They went down the Mount of Olives at Goodenough's usual speed, which was not based on such considerations as the view, or the nerves either, of Jerusalem, and brought up presently in a cloud of dust in front of a marquee behind a barbed-wire fence on the outskirts of the city. Two minutes later Narayan Singh, lean, enormous, bearded, looked straight into his colonel's eyes across the table.

"You're to go with this officer, Narayan Singh."

"*Atcha, sahib.*"

"You're to bring him back from Ludd alive."

"*Atcha, sahib.*"

"Otherwise do whatever he tells you to."

"*Atcha,* colonel *sahib.*"

"March with your kit to the station and meet Major Grim there in time for the morning train. Dismiss."

The Sikh saluted and fell away, but his brown eyes met Jim's with a flare of gratitude. It was almost ferocious, like the expression of a hound unchained for sport. Jim nodded to him, but neither said a word.

Jim borrowed the colonel's car and drove to the junior staff officer's mess, where he went upstairs in a hurry. Finding nobody in his own room, he went on up to the attic and stooped over an enormous packing-case. Groping in it, he pulled out a black foot, followed by a small boy, whose wooly hair suggested the Sudan and a mother sold into Arab slavery. His features were certainly Arabic.

"You lucky, lucky little devil! Twelve hours' sleep out of twenty-four—just think of it! Wake up now and pack you kit; roll it into your blanket and come with me to the station."

"What is it, Jimgrim? Are we transferred?"

"You've got to learn to ask no questions when you get your marching-orders."

"All right, Jimgrim."

"Narayan Singh will inspect that kit when you get to the station. Better be careful."

He left the boy sleepily arranging on a blanket all the odds and ends that had appealed to his eight-year-old imagination since Jim discovered him starving one winter night in the drafty archway of the Jaffa Gate. They were pretty much the same things that a small boy born in America would choose—a tine can, a broken knife, a mouth-organ, a picture out of a magazine, an incomplete pack of playing cards, some half-smoked cigarettes and a broken mousetrap—all frightfully important.

Jim packed into his own kit three complete changes of native costume, and was ready first.

Narayan Singh was the only one of Jim's friends who did not object to Suliman; the only one who took it for granted that the profit of fostering a small boy might outweigh the trouble, and who was thoroughly willing to share the trouble and forego all profit.

The Sikh took charge of Suliman at the station, made him unroll his kit on the platform, rebuked him because the broken knife-blade was not clean, solemnly suggested proper ways of polishing the outside of a tine box, and invent on the spot the only moral and properly complicated way of packing such possessions in a blanket.

In the flat-wheeled train that bumped and pounded through the gorge leading down from Jerusalem Narayan Singh came forward from the third-class end of the train to find Jim.

"The *butcha* will make a man, *sahib*," he announced.

"Why, what's his latest?"

"I asked him what he supposes our *sahib* intends to do with him at Ludd.

"'Though I could hide in your beard, Narayan Singh,' he said, 'and you have killed your man a dozen times, yet I shall be a soldier before you are. For though you do not know enough not know enough not to ask questions when you have had marching orders, nevertheless I know enough not to answer you.' How is that, *sahib*, from a *butcha* hardly higher than my knee?"

"He learns. But see he doesn't smoke too much, and when he swears beat him."

* * * *

Brigadier-General Jenkins was on the station-platform at Ludd, cutting quite a figure, what with his upstanding bulk and the number of obedient subalterns grouped all about him. The set stage was obvious at once. The administrator's motor had evidently come faster than the train. Jenkins had been ordered to accept an apology, and for lack of any better means of showing spite had arranged to make it as public as possible.

Jim, with Narayan Singh at his heels carrying all the baggage, walked straight up to him and saluted.

"Well, Major Grim?"

"I apologize."

Jenkins turned a little to one side in order better to include the crowd.

"What for?"

"For presuming to speak to you as a man and my equal the other day instead of as a person of higher rank. I withdraw all I said, including the imputation. Do you accept?"

Jenkins nodded. Having his orders from higher up, it was all he could do. The subalterns smirked as he turned on his heel, and two or three of them winked at Jim. Narayan Singh was the only one who spoke, growling into Jim's ear as he once more gathered up the baggage:

"Lead on, Jimgrim, *sahib*. I have seen the day when stronger board than that one bit the dust!"

CHAPTER II

"That was only an American devil. This is a Palestine one. They are much worse."

There is one good thing, at any rate, about being commissioned under army regulations. It is true that you have to concede gentility to seniors sometimes ignorant of the crudest meaning of the word; but on the other hand you yourself remain a presumptive gentleman until the contrary is proven. You are liable to arrest at the whim of arrogance; but you don't have to find bail, or sit in a cell until your case comes up for hearing.

So Jim found Catesby taking it easy in a deckchair in his tent—a pretty good tent, nicely hung with souvenirs of the East from Cairo to Bokhara, with soda-water siphons in a basket full of wet grass slung from the ridge-pole in the sun to keep them cool, and plenty to read.

"Hullo, Uncle Sam. What are you doing here? Come in. Make yourself at home. I heard you were under arrest in Jeroosh."

"No. I apologized."

"Lucky devil. Wish an apology might fumigate my official rep. Afraid I'm damned. How on earth did you manage it? Jinks had been bragging all over the shop that he'd as good as broke you. Mother of me! D'you mean to say you're at liberty and camping on Jinks' trail? Oh—what was that word of Roosevelt's—oh, bully! Jimgrim, if you get Jenkins' number I'll pledge myself to black your boots from now to doomsday."

"My orders are to whitewash him."

"Oh, damn! That means good-by me. Howe for me on a troopship to what used to be Merrie England—broke."

"Incidentally, I've orders to clear you."

"Can't be done, old man; not if the impeccable Jinks is to save his face. They tell me *sub rosa* that he's cooking up half a dozen extra charges to make sure of breaking me."

"Business is business," Jim chuckled. "All this firm asks is orders. Goods delivered while you wait."

"But listen; we haven't an earthly. Two tons of TNT came in a truck consigned by mistake to this brigade. The R.T.O. (railway man) shot it into a sliding and notified Jinks, who probably lost the advice or lit his pipe with it.

"Three days later the Air Force, who were expecting the stuff, began to make inquires—twisted the tail of the R.T.O. to help his memory—went to the siding—found the truck—seals broken—no TNT. Went to Jinks promptly. Jinks blustered as usual—denied all knowledge of the consignment—was shown a copy of the R.T.O's memorandum—remembered a few stale grudges against me, and swore he had give me orders to go and take charge of the stuff the moment it came. I was sent for, and it was the first I'd heard of it.

"In less than two minutes he had me under arrest to await court martial for culpable negligence and disobedience to orders. I shall plead not guilty, of course. He'll swear he gave me orders. I'll deny it. His word against mine. *Maalesh*—feenish!—as the Arabs say."

"What other charges can he bring against you?"

"Anything he pleases. What's the odds? There's so much thieving going on in this camp—no thieves caught or stuff re-covered—that any sort of charge against anyone gets believed. How can you possibly checkmate a brigadier like Jenkins in the circumstances?"

"Did you ever kill a dog?" asked Jim.

"Yes."

"How?"

"Bullet. Poison. Why?"

"They say there are more ways of killing them than by chok-ing them to death with butter; but suppose we try butter just this once."

"Jinks'll eat all the butter there is and yell for more."

"Let's try him. Tell me what you know, or guess, or think, about that TNT. You know I've discovered the stuff in Jerusalem? There was a Moslem plot to blow up the Dome of the Rock and blame it on the Zionists. Who's the worst fanatic in these parts?"

"All the Hebron men are fanatics; you know that. They're the principal thieves. They hide all over the place, and grease themselves at night, and slip past the sentries. Once in a while one gets skewered with a bayonet or shot, but the look outweighs the risk, and for one that gets napooed twenty get away with it."

"Kettle told me it looked like organized conspiracy."

"I don't believe it. It's just half-brother Ishmael with his hand against every man and every man's hand against him."

"You haven't heard of any sheik or priest or trader hereabouts who's getting rich and uppish?"

"No. It's simply a case of flies around a jam-pot."

"See you later," said Jim, grinning to hide from Catesby his own appreciation of the fact that the brigadier held all the trump cards.

He continued to wear the grin by way of self-encouragement.

* * * *

Every circumstance, condition, situation and characteristic has its advantage, only so few know how to look for them. Still, a more than normally alert man can stumble on advantage now and then; and if he has trained himself he can sometimes make the most of what turns up. Individuals seem to have special values in the eternal scheme. The especial merit of Suliman was that, being a small boy, he hero-worshiped and at the same time believed implicitly in bogies.

The merit of a Sikh is different. He, too, worships heroes, but from another point of view; and the more he happens to believe in the unseen, the more suspicious he is of the unexplainable that can be seen and touched and heard. But this both Sikhs and small boys have in common, that they love the lines and the gossip of the lines.

Narayan Singh, given no orders to the contrary, could not more have kept away from the tents where other Sikhs were idling the time away that Suliman could have done, orders to the contrary of not.

Jim went to the row of tents reserved for visiting officers, discovered his bed already made and kit unpacked, but nothing of Narayan Singh or Suliman. There was a Sikh mounting guard at either end of the short line, but they knew no more than that Narayan Singh had come and gone again, taking the *butcha* with him. So he set off to explore the camp on his own accord.

Ludd, which was Lystra when they wrote the Bible, is one of those places that fills the military mind with wonder at civilian complacency, and stirs civilians to murmur at the thoughtlessness of army men. The town itself is practically undefendable. Yet there has always been a town there, in a land where raid and robbery are the normal thing; and wherever Jew, Egyptian, Philistine, Syrian, Babylonian, Roman, Mongol, crusader and Turk in turn have razed the place, its inhabitants have always built it up again very much as ants rebuild a ruined hill.

It sits on a sandy plain at the foot of the Judean Hills, from which plunderers can swoop down on it at their discretion. There is practically no water except in the rainy season, when there is a lot too much. There are snakes, mosquitoes, centipedes, bedbugs, fleas and flies. And the largest army in the Near East was camped there, drawing its drinking-water all the way from Egypt through an iron pipe made in the U.S.A.

The secret of that is that, although the surrounding hills are perfectly contrived by nature to be robbers' fastnesses, and the plains below were manifestly meant for robbers' meat, you can't supply and maneuver an army readily among the hills, whereas Ludd is not only a railway junction but is an excellent pushing-off place in every direction, with ample room for store-sheds, airplanes, cavalry lines and what not. So the army, depending on mobility for its security, tolerated the climate and conditions, while the thieves descended from places in the hills, like Hebron, and grew fat.

Jim strolled about the camp enjoying himself more or less, as any man must who loves with devouring interest whatever lives. In an armed camp the very gun-mules learn a new intelligence; and the dogs, without which in dozens no British army—or

American for that matter—could maintain its social self-respect, come nearer to being impudently human than in any other circumstances.

There is tidiness, even among barbed-wire and prickly-pear entanglements, and a sense of getting the very utmost out of life (which is true humor as well as sound economy) that may become monotonous to those in camp, but thrill the new arrivals. And there are all the minor innovations made by individual commanding officers for making something out of nothing for the men's sake, to be admired, or criticized, if you are half-observant. Nothing much escaped Jim's eye or missed its lodgment in his memory. But there was nothing that looked like a cord for hanging Jenkins.

At the end of an hour of all-observant sauntering he returned to the station to interview the R.T.O., a red-necked, overworked, opinionative despot (like the rest of them; it seems you can't run a military railway and be tolerant of other people's feelings). Someone in the early days of war had dug this man out from a freight-junction in a London suburb, put him in uniform, and he had done the rest. He did not mind who knew it.

"Ho! So you're another that wants to know about that TNT? I told all I knew the minute they asked me. Facts at my fingers' ends. Made my report in writing. Nothing more to say!"

But there are ways of getting under the thick skin even of an R.T.O.

"How much truth is there in the story that you get commissions from the thieves who loot the railway?"

"What, me? Who says that? Hell's bells! This gang'ud accuse their wet-nurse of selling milk! Anything missing? Blame the R.T.O.! Horse breaks away—sepoy get a dose of colic—general lose his shaving-brush? Require explanations in triplicate from the R.T.O.! Train two minutes late? Arrest the R.T.O. for mutiny! That's the life I lead.

"Listen. That TNT arrived in a truck. None o' my business. I ain't the hen that laid the stuff. I wrote out an advice on the proper form and sent it up to Jenkins, ordered the truck into number nineteen siding, and says to myself, 'There, that's the end of that, God damn it!' and as far as I'm concerned that *is* the end of it. I'm busy. But if there's a man in Palestine from general downwards who wants to swap me two piasters against all the commissions I get from thieves or anyone, walk him up to my office and we'll make the trade. *Good* morning!"

There was nothing to be unearthed there. The man was obviously as honest as self-satisfied. Jim strolled back to the camp and through the mule-transport lines, where he found Narayan Singh squatting on the sand in deep converse with a dozen grooms. Six or seven tents away Suliman was smoking a cigarette and gambling with three Arab urchins of about his own age.

He caught Narayan Singh's eye and nodded, passing on without disturbing the group to pounce on Suliman, turn him upside down and shake him until the unearthed increment of small coins fell into the sand to be fought for by the other three.

"But not all that money was won from them!" Suliman objected.

"Good. Teach you not to gamble."

* * * *

Suliman had to run to keep up and lost breath in the process for the sand made heavy going. But he talked all the way, remonstrating at first about the loss of all that wit-won money, and, when remonstrance failed to produce the least effect, forgetting it in an intermittent flow of gossip. That being exactly what Jim wanted, there began to be abrupt replies that brought forth more.

"And, Jimgrim, this Ludd must be an evil place, although I like the mules and horses and dogs and men and everything."

"Well, what's the matter with it, then?"

"There is an *iblis*."

"A devil, is there? What does the devil do?"

"He is captain of the thieves. He dances at night in the hills, and the thieves bring him what they steal. He is *abras*."

"A leper is he? Have to start to P.M.O. on his trail."

"No. They say the chief doctor is afraid of him."

"Why?"

"Because besides being *abras* he is *mukaddas*."

"Holy, eh?"

"He is a *derwish* (dervish). They say he bewitches men by dancing, and after that the sentries can't see to shoot them or kill them with bayonets. I am afraid of the *iblis* Jimgrim. You will have to let me sleep inside your tent, because it is too dangerous outside under the sky."

"Tell me some more about the *iblis*. What is his name?"

"They say he has no name."

"Where does he live?"

"Nowhere—that is, everywhere! He comes and goes—first men see him in one place, then in another. They say he wears no clothes except a turban, and has beastly great marks of leprosy all over him. They say that if a soldier sees him, he can never shoot straight again, and when a man touches him, that man dies within the day. Oh, Jimgrim, suppose he should come in the night!"

Jim sat down on the "deckchair, officer's one" provided by a thoughtful War Office, and grinned.

"You've given me the right idea, youngster. Just for gambling you shall investigate this *iblis*."

"Allah forbid! I would not even go with you to look at him!"

"All right. Then you shall wear girl's clothes for a year."

"*Aib! Ana bkul la!* (Shame! I say no!) Rather I will promise never to gamble again."

"You've promised before. You have gambled again. Now you've got to choose—forward like a man to find the *iblis*, or a girl's clothes for twelve months."

"I could run away to some village, Jimgrim. You would never find me."

"Suit yourself."

"When you were my age, Jimgrim, would you have gone to look for an *iblis*?"

"Sure."

"*Kizzab mutkarbik!* (You are a big liar!)"

"I hunted one before I was your age and found it was made of a pumpkin, a beanpole and a sheet."

"That was only an American devil. This is a Palestine one. They are much worse."

"Nothing's bad unless you're afraid of it," said Jim.

"Not gambling? I am not afraid of that."

"But you're afraid of the consequences—girl's clothes for a year."

Suliman stamped his foot and swore a steady stream of brimstone Arabic.

"Remember, you're only allowed ten swears a day!"

"I am a man! I will not wear a girl's clothes!"

"You'll find the *iblis* is a man when you lay hold of him."

"How can that be?"

"That's for you to find out."

At that moment Narayan Singh arrived silently, and saluted in the tent door.

"All the camp is by the ears about a *shaitan* (devil), *sahib*. He is said to make thieves invisible and to cast a spell on soldiers so that they can never shoot or stab straight."

"So I hear."

"They say he may not be hunted because Moslems think his person is sacred. They say, too, he is a leper; yet the medical officer may not arrest him for the same reason. Yet some say he is captain of the thieves. Shall we two take him in hand?"

"Sure. First thing."

"Does your honor want him alive? What if I put his sacredness to the test with a bullet?"

"Better investigate him first; there may be others. Be ready to come with me after dark.

"*Atcha, sahib*. Shall I place Suliman with friends who will look after him?"

"*La!* (No)" yelled Suliman. "I am a better man that any Sikh! I tell you I go too!"

CHAPTER III

"Now I won't hear a word from you against Jenkins—not one word!"

From a cursory inspection of that camp, such as any ordinary visitor might give it, the impression would have been gained that Brigadier-General Jenkins was supreme. That was because his brigade command chance to lie nearest to the station, and his notion of the only way to achieve success in life was through advertisement.

Like many a commercial upstart of the type that he admired, advertisement had done a lot for him, and presently turned his head. To carry the metaphor further, he was becoming "overextended," pyramiding "futures" on the sudden profits of a chancy past. There were others than the administrator in Jerusalem aware of his ambition and the meager grounds for it.

For instance, there was Major-General Anthony V.C. etc., in supreme command at Ludd, whom the public had hardly ever heard of because he cared to serve his country only, not himself. Jim found him in his shirt sleeves in the great marquee that overlooked the whole camp from rising ground at the rear.

"Glad to see you, Grim. Sit down. General Kettle was here this morning. He gave you some orders himself, I believe?"

"I've apologized already."

"Good. You're in my bad books, though. I was absent in Egypt when that TNT was lost. That gave Jenkins a chance to shift the blame, and he made the most of it. Now, thanks to your recovering the stuff and your block-headed idiocy in falling foul of him, Jenkins get a new lease.

"Between you and me, Grim, he is one of those damned politicians. Friends in the War Office, you know, and all that kind of thing.

"There seems no way of getting rid of him. He reached his present eminence by being recommended for promotion by one C.O. after another, who couldn't endure him by didn't want to quarrel with his powerful friends.

"His career is on long story of innocent fellows punished or broke to hide his shortcomings. Now, thanks to your infernal hot temper, he looks like breaking poor young Catesby, who's an efficient young officer.

"You're the logical man to have followed up that TNT business. You had it in hand and were successful beyond expectation. If you'd held your idiotic tongue, instead of telling Jenkins what you thought of him, I could have turned you loose down here, and what with his dislike of you and your brains I don't doubt he'd have tripped himself out of the Army in a week or so.

"But imagine what a whip hand it would give Jenkins over me if it transpired that I had proceeded against him on charges brought by a major who had been ordered to apologize to him for insubordination only a few days before! Do you see what your hotheadedness has done?

"Now I won't hear a word from you against Jenkins—not one word! You're to investigate the thieving that's going on down here, but I shall make a point of telling Jenkins myself this afternoon that you are here in his interest as much as anyone's.

"Now—is there anything I can do to simplify matters for you in any way?"

"I ought to have Catesby's assistance, sir."

"But he's under arrest."

"Catesby needs time and opportunity to hunt up evidence in his own defense, sir."

"He has made no such request to me. If would have to come from him, not you."

"I'm his next friend. If it comes to a court martial I shall defend him."

"I see. You propose to ignore my wigging and fall foul of the brigadier in that way, don't you?"

"Absolutely no, sir! I'll carry out your orders to the letter."

"All right; I'll trust you. A note shall go to Jenkins asking him to release Captain Catesby's parole for fourteen days to enable him to look up evidence. Anything else?"

"You've heard of the *iblis*, of course?"

"The leper who dances in the moonlight? Yes. He's quite a problem. I was for having him hunted and bagged alive. The P.M.O. wants him interned as a danger to the health of the whole neighborhood, though where the hell he'd intern him I don't know. But some politician has been pulling strings. It seems the leper is a religious mystic held in high regard by the Moslems, and orders have come that he's not to be interfered with."

"They say in the lines that this *iblis* is the captain of the thieves."

"I know they do. I've known of things ten times more im-probable."

"In that case," said Jim, "whatever politician pulled the strings is probably interested in the thieving."

"The order to let the leper alone came from Egypt."

"Why not override it on the ground of military expediency?"

"Because, the war's over, Grim, and the politicians are getting the upper hand. The way is being paved for civil government, and for every once that I override the political department I get ten defeats. I'm disposed now to let the politicians mix their own litter and lie in it."

Jim was a lot too wise to ask permission after that to tackle the *iblis*. It was sufficient that he had no orders not to tackle him. But he was more mystified than ever. Just as Sir Henry Kettle had done that morning, General Anthony seemed to be deliberately leaving the course unobstructed which, if Jim could find it, might lead to Jenkins' undoing. Why in thunder couldn't they tackle Jenkins outright, he wondered.

* * * *

He went straight to Jenkins' ten and sent his name in by the orderly, but was kept waiting five minutes while the brigadier whistled a tune; for there is nothing like cooling a junior's heels, according to some folk.

"Can you tell me anything, sir, that might lead to the discovery of who stole the TNT?" he asked when he was admitted.

"Hah! So our wonderful, astute American has come for assistance, eh? I thought you were such an expert intelligence officer that you never needed anyone's advice? Glad to come to me after all, eh? What anticlimax! I dare say you wish now you'd made that apology a little more humble and less technical?"

There was no one else in the tent, although there might have been some eavesdropper listening behind it, for Jenkins knew no limits when his own advantage was in question. Jim took a grip on himself, and smiled.

"I've been rebuked twice this morning for what I said to you the other day. Twice I've pledged myself to make amends, if I can, buy getting all possible credit for you out of the clearing up of this thieving business."

"Oh!"

If there was one thing more than another on which Brigadier-General Jenkins prided himself it was his ability to read men and take advantage of their peculiarities. Next to that he considered his claim to success lay in swift appraisal of subsurface reasons—political judgement in other words.

Jim Grim he assessed as one of those slaved of integrity, who value their own word above all other considerations; a slave, moreover, who had no influential backing. He did not doubt that whatever Jim had promised to do he would do, whoever might be discommoded in the process. There were only two men who could have made Jim promise—Kettle and Anthony—and only someone higher up still who could have actuated them; therefore somebody attached to headquarters in Cairo must have been pulling more than usually effective strings.

There might even have come definite instructions from the Foreign Office in London that the way must be paved for Brigadier-General Jenkins' appointment to a civil post. The day of civil government was rapidly approaching. He himself had worked all the backstairs wires. There were more unlikely things.

Jenkins was no simpleton. He understood perfectly that both Kettle and Anthony detested and despised him; and, blinded by his own conceit, he supposed they would be willing to praise him with their tongues in their cheeks in order to get rid of him.

"Soho!" he remarked, and whistled a bar or two.

Jim, loathing him, skin, bone and stuffing, stood with a straight face, waiting while the brigadier turned his stalwart back to think.

"So we're to pull together, are we, eh? Well—I'm not vindictive. I'd half a mind to ruin your career—d'you know that? I won't stand insolence from any man. *Nemo me impune lacessit*; that's my motto. I've got teeth, and I like the world to know it. However, as you seem eager to reinforce a lame apology by doing the right thing, I'll bet bygones be bygones and we'll forget the incident."

Jim's memory was reputed to be a trifle more retentive that that, had Jenkins stopped to think, but the brigadier was full steam ahead already on the track of self-advancement with the terminus in view. The brakes weren't working.

"Sit down. Now this thieving that has been going on in the camp is a perfectly scandalous business. There's no excuse for it. Not counting that TNT, which was returned to store—thanks to some extent, I believe to your efforts—the Army has lost a hundred and nine rifles in three months, to say nothing of countless rounds of ammunition—blankets—groceries—soap—underclothing—and stores of all kinds. Incompetence, of course. Best not to mention names.

"Between you and me, I've been waiting for the Army auditor to check things up and discover how much is missing. That's done now. They know in Cairo just how much remissness there has been.

"Now's the time, then, for somebody to get credit for changing that state of affairs. You're a man who's had rapid promotion; there's no need to tell you that the paving of the short cut consists of other men's mistakes. Very well. Somebody will have to pay; but what is that man's poison may turn out to be your meat and mine. D'you get my meaning?"

"Perfectly."

"Have a cigar. It's obvious to the meanest intelligence—or at least it ought to be obvious, you'd think—that these thieves have a headquarters. Any general with half an eye would recognize sings of the thieves being organized. That means they've got a leader—perhaps two or three men, but more likely one—directing all of them. Is that much clear?"

"Sounds obvious."

"It is. My notion of a good commanding office is a man with his ear to the ground, who listens, and knows what the men are saying. Any man with only one ear, and that half full of wax, would know that it's common talk in this camp that the captain of thieves is a notorious leper. Have you heard of him?"

"Yes."

"Have you heard any reasonable explanation as to why he's left at liberty? No, of course you haven't, for there is none. There's a reason given, of course, but it's childish. They're afraid of offending the Moslems. Now listen to me."

"Go ahead. I'm listening."

"Have a drink. Help yourself. Now who would stand to gain most by stealing weapons? Eh? Who are they who want to possess a country owned by present by Arabs—who are being threatened everlastingly by Arabs—who have no weapons of their own, and whose grip on the country is only made temporarily possible by an army of occupation dependent on the whims of a Foreign Office? The Zionists, eh? D'you get me?"

"Then you mean—"

"I mean this: The Arabs have lots of weapons hidden away. The Zionists have none—or had none until this thieving started. The Zionists believe, what I'm quite sure of, that they're going to get left in the lurch by our Foreign Office sooner or later. So they've hired Arabs to steal rifles for them, for Jews to use against Arabs later on. D'you follow me?"

"I see the drift."

"Kettle and Anthony and the rest of them imagine that the Zionists are going to have it all their own way with the backing of the British Government. But I know better. I happen to have influential connections at home who keep me posted; and between you and me the Zionists are going to be told before long to paddle their own canoe.

"Of course, the Zionists have their own friends at the Foreign Office, who keep them posted, too; they know as well as you and

I do what's likely to happen, and that the minute it does they'll be at the mercy of the Arabs unless they can arm themselves in advance. Failing arms, they'll have to get out of the country. That's inevitable finally; they'll have to get out. You can take my word for it, the solution of this Palestine problem is going to be an Arab kingdom. The Zionists haven't a chance."

Jim saw no reason to argue with a man who chose to back a losing horse. He sat still.

"I rather think General Anthony himself suspects this thieving is the work of Zionists," Jenkins went on. "But he's afraid of Zionists, as well as more than half in favor of them. I'm not. I know which side my bread is buttered on, and I'm pro-Arab to the core. Are you?"

"I'm extremely partial to Arabs," Jim answered guardedly. "Can't help liking them."

"So we'll just take a fall out of the Zionists ahead of time, and let the Arabs know who their individual friends are, with an eye to the future. Get after that *iblis*, as they call him, Grim, as soon as you like. Scratch him and I think you'll find a Jew; if not, you'll discover a Jew somewhere back of him."

"I thought of getting on his trail tonight," said Jim.

"Good. Do. Report to me and to no one else. See you in the morning, then. So long."

* * * *

Ten minutes later Jim turned up at Catesby's tent.

"No 'home on a tropper' for you, old man! This Jenkins bird is going to provide you with work."

"But you've got to whitewash the brute!"

"Sure. The Lord alone knows how yet, but he shall have such an elegant ducking in white paint that it won't ever come off. Your parole's to be raised for fourteen days, and we'll work together to pump Jinks so full of self-importance that he'll burst. Meanwhile, I'll get some sleep. You do the same. Don't forget, if anybody asks, that you need liberty to hunt up evidence to clear yourself. So long."

CHAPTER IV

"Moreover, Jimgrim, you are my friend!"

No city in the world can vie with a great camp for binding spells, by night especially; for the city only represents what men have done, whereas the camp allures with what they mean to do. The policeman at a crossing signifies that what today approves tomorrow will repeat. The sentry with firelight dancing on his pointed steel denotes the alertness of unfolding destiny. The entertainment of a city is the fruit of things accomplished, growing rotten, but the thrilling murmur of a camp by night is the prelude to new heavens and a new earth.

There was no moon when Jim led the way between the whickering horse-lines, followed by Catesby, Narayan Singh and Suliman. They were all dressed as Arabs, so that every sentry challenged them, and once a bayonet point pierced through Jim's garments to his skin before he could reply; for the Sikh on duty likes his ceremony swift, and takes no chances.

Each time that Jim whispered the password the four were followed into the shadows by wondering, suspicious eyes; then, as if afterthought increased suspicion, the sentry's voice would call out harshly to the next ahead, and three times before they reached the camp gate an officer was fetched to quiz them.

In no single instance did Jim give the names of his party, not even when the guard at the gap in a barb wire fence that they called the south gate held them up for five minutes and scoffed at the slip of paper he produced. He did not want his movements gossiped all over the camp. SO they were all four submitted to search at the gate as presumptive thieves, by a Sikh *jemadar* who feared no writing nor regarded words.

His disrespectful fingers uncovered naturally three loaded automatic pistols; and—ace of unexpectedness—a Gurkha kukri from under Suliman's shirt. That settled it, of course.

"Into the lock-up with them until morning!" he ordered, being one of those priceless guardians who are not afraid of responsibility.

"The luck's not running my way," grunted Catesby. "This'll give Jinks the finest chance the brute could ask for to show me up in a bad light. My name's Walker!"

"Don't you believe it. Cut loose, Narayan Singh," Jim whispered.

There followed an interlude in the Jat dialect that restored Catesby's normal high spirits, it being one of the conventions of the British Army that an officer of Sikhs must understand the language of his men, whereas the men's knowledge of English is optional and rather rare. It ended in Narayan Singh disrobing in the guardroom light to show his steel bracelet, the steel dagger in his hair, and certain other peculiarities of Sikh attire to which he is more loyal than a Scotsman to his kilts. Those, the language, and an intimate knowledge of he *jemadar's* own personal, private and amusing immortal history proved at last convincing.

But the *jemadar* kept the kukri. There was not explaining that away.

"How shall I hunt an *iblis* without that thing?" demanded Suliman, appealing to Jim in the shadow much too wise to argue with the Sikh.

"Where did you get it? Did a Gurkha lend it to you?"

"No. The fool refused. So I stole it while he drank."

"Come on. We've wasted time enough. You must face the *iblis* with bare hands."

* * * *

Now Catesby led, for he knew the lie of the land. Jim followed him, and Narayan Singh brought up the rear in darkness so deep that it was all one could do to keep the leading man in sight. The sky overhead was clear, and the stars shone like scattered diamonds, but they were following a shallow *wady* (valley) between cactus, and the gloom of the night before the worlds were made seemed to have gathered in it. They went nearly a mile at a slow pace before Catesby stopped to take his bearings. Then Jim missed Suliman.

He did not dare shout for him, for that would have brought to the scene every scrub-haunting thief in the neighborhood. He called once in a low voice, but all the answer was the ghoul-like laugh of a hyena, and a moment later he made out the brute's green eyes, very low to the ground and moving the way a lantern swings.

"I rather thought it was a mistake to bring that kid," said Catesby. "Didn't like to question your judgement of course, but—"

"He comes. I hear him, *sahib*," Narayan Singh whispered.

A moment later the hyena snarled and scampered off, looking as big as a lion when his outline showed against the sky. Then they heard whimpering and hard breathing. Something or somebody stumbled, sobbed, and hurried on again toward them. Then Suliman burst into their midst and threw himself face foremost on the earth, heaving for lack of breath. He had something heavy in his hand. Jim picked it up.

"The kukri again! You young *luss* (robber)! How did you get it?"

"That *jemadar* gave it to a sentry to hold, and the sentry laid it beside him on the ground where he could feel it with his foot. So I pulled the skirt of his overcoat and took the kukri when he turned. Then I ran."

"And he didn't shoot?"

"No, for I took care that he saw me. Silks don't shoot at men of my size, for I have tried before."

"Now," said Jim, do you still think I was wrong to bring the kid? Lead on, Catesby."

* * * *

They took to the top of a sandy ridge that lead gradually upward to a low hill covered with cactus, from which by daylight there would be a fair view of half the camp, although now they could see little more than scattered lights that made the darkness more confusing. There was a short bare ridge on the hilltop, sandy like the rest but free from cactus.

"Suppose we lie here till moonrise," Catesby proposed. "Last time I saw the *iblis* was from just this place. I was waiting for a chance at a leopard and friend leper came instead, scaring everything away for miles around. He pretty nearly scared me stiff. Most awful looking brute you ever saw.

"You see that hill opposite? You can just make out the outline of it against the sky. He danced on that and made me feel so creepy I vowed I'd never dance again. Later he passed along this ridge so close that I thought he'd trip over me. Ugh! I was glad he didn't. He's leprous from head to foot. It beats me how he holds together when he dances."

They lay down on a shoulder of sand that overhung the shallow valley; and now the Arab costume they were wearing proved its virtue, for they could cover faces, hands and ankles from the mosquitoes that attacked in mass formation. Hooded like that under loose robes they looked like dead men. A badger came and sniffed them, then a hyena, then several jackals, remembering perhaps the fat times when men were fighting and the carrion lay thick.

They lay an hour until the moon rose, like a huge blotched lamp beyond the other hill, and by that time Suliman was fast asleep and snoring. Narayan Singh shook him awake—lest he frighten the *iblis* away, as the Sikh was careful to explain. The notion that the *iblis* might be afraid of himself was new to Suliman, and he sat up to consider it, fingering the edge of the heavy, curved Gurkha blade.

"The game is to catch this beauty alive if we can," said Jim, "but above all we mustn't scare him and let him get away from us. Better watch him for a week than rush in and fail. The next most important thing is not to kill him—bear that in mind, Narayan Singh; even you can't make a dead man talk, you know!"

"I will plunge this kukri in his belly and discover whether an *iblis* has entrails if he comes near me!" vowed Suliman.

But a moment later he returned the great knife to its sheath and crept up close to Jim, with the hair raising so that his turban actually lifted.

"Look, Jimgrim! Look! The *iblis!*"

Naked in the reddish moonlight—framed, in fact, exactly in the middle of the orb that rose behind him, about two hundred yards distant from where they lay across the *wady*—glistening here and there as if his carcass had been smeared with whitish slime, a tall, lean, muscular man stood motionless, gazing toward the lights that indicated Ludd encampment.

The turban on his head but emphasized the nakedness of all the rest of him. Nowhere in the East is the mere absence of clothes remarkable as a rule, although the Arab likes to drape himself in amble, loose array for the sake of dignity and comfort. But the man's nakedness was ghastly—impudent—a calculated, sheer affront—deliberate indecency so flaunted that the moonlight and the loneliness could not absorb it, and it shocked grown men.

He was well shaped. No crippled limbs or unnatural abortion helped to horrify. It was an arrogance of nakedness, made monstrous by the will to assert itself. If he had stood among a hundred naked men, he alone would have seemed unclothed, and if you had clothed him he might likely have seemed naked still because of the outrageous insolence that owned him.

For minute after minute he stood gazing at the camp, with his stomach thrust out in an attitude of self-complacency and his arms folded across his chest. Then, as if the turban on his head were too much concession to the prejudice of other folk, he began to unwind the thing, coiling the yards of cloth around his arm.

"What did I tell you?" whispered Catesby. "Isn't he a horror? Isn't he a gruesome swine?"

"In my land there are millions with no more than a yard or two of rag apiece; but that thing there is an insult to the gods, and he should die!" declared Narayan Singh.

"Nevertheless, remember what I said. Don't kill him," Jim answered. "He thinks he knows something or he wouldn't like himself so much. Let's find out."

The man began to posture on the hilltop, taking attitudes suggestive of the figures on Egyptian temple walls. He seemed conscious of the fact that the rising moon served to spotlight as well as background, for his movements were deliberately calculated to show up in silhouette. They were slow and strong and snakelike, but little by little the snake idea gained ascendancy until his whole body writhed in serpentine contortions.

Then he began to dance. You could not watch the man and tear yourself away or make a move against him. He had the faculty of stirring curiosity and holding it, so that each move was a fascinating prelude to the next and you had to wait to see.

The dance began with a rapid repetition of the Egyptian poses, so skillfully done that the infinitely tiny pause between each movement served to fix each posture in the watchers' vision, and the whole became a motion picture in staccato time.

All that while he kept the turban draped about his arm and it looked like an excrescence—something or other horrible—sometimes as if he had three arms on his right side, two growing out of one. But all at once he began to whirl the thing about him like a lariat until it formed a Saturn ring, in the midst of which he spun like a top on tiptoe, dervish fashion.

Whoever on the countryside saw that would understand the meaning of it. The whirling turban was only an added stroke of genius to emphasize his eminence among his kind.

The dancing dervish claims that by spinning for a length of time on tiptoe he can rid himself of human limitations and see clearly into the infinite. The ordinary dervish apes an arrogant humility before he starts; this fellow was assuming to confer with spiritual essences with banner whirling in the breeze—that was the only difference. There might be Moslems after that who would question his claim to miraculous vision and sanctity, but not many of them, and hey would be kept in order by the rest.

Suliman, with the creed of his ancestors half-learned and wholly in his veins, was quite convinced.

"That is truly an *iblis*," he whispered with chattering teeth. "There is nothing for us to do but leave him, Jimgrim."

But Jim was thinking then too busily to quiet the superstitious qualms of a small boy.

"Narayan Singh!"

The Sikh crept closer.

"Do you know the lie of the land here?"

"No, *sahib*. But I could crawl up close and rush the brute. If I may not slay, I could hold him until you come and bind him with the turban."

"Catesby!"

The three laid their heads together.

"Is there any way of coming up behind him?"

"No. Not without making a circuit of more than a mile. This hill we're on juts out from a ridge that leads in a curve to his hill. There's a thirty-foot cliff of sand on this side of him, too steep to climb in the dark. If we follow the ridge he'd see us coming, unless we could get there before he stops spinning, and at that he has likely got a spy or two on the watch. To come up from behind him through the cactus would take twenty minutes."

"Jimgrim, *sahib!*"

Narayan Singh laid a hand on Jim's sleeve.

"If I steady this automatic on my forearm," the Sikh continued, "resting my elbow on the ground—thus—in three or four shots I can hit him in the leg with certainty. Then he will limp, and we can catch him. Only say the word."

"No."

"The last time I saw him he came straight along the ridge and passed me after he'd finished the ballet," whispered Catesby.

"Give him a chance to do it again."

The *iblis* pirouetted interminably, gaining rather than losing speed, the ring of cloth spreading out around him in an ever widening circle. If he really was a leper, then the disease had made strangely little inroad on his stamina.

And for all that whoever watched grew giddy, the *iblis* himself retained full consciousness. For there came cloaked figures of men, who dodged in the shadows from bush to bush; and as they drew near he was aware of them and began to slow down gradually, letting the turban droop in ever narrowing curves, until he stood stock-still again, back to the moon, like a statue, glistening with sweat that made him shine now from head to foot instead of showing sliminess in patches.

After standing rigid for about two minutes he stretched out his right arm toward the camp, and suddenly his voice boomed like a tenor bell, cursing in Arabic, cursing in the name of Allah the Lord of Creatures, the Prince of the Day of Judgment, cursing man and beast and tent and mechanism—eye, hand, ear and brain.

"What do you make of him?" he whispered.

"I've seen his kind in the mosques of Mosul and Marash," Catesby whispered. "I think he's simply a dancing dervish from up north, driven away very likely because of his leprosy."

But Jim, too, had been in Mosul and Marash and seen the dancing dervishes. He reserved judgment.

The *iblis* turned at last toward the hooded figures that were crouching near him; and now he stretched out both arms, but whether or not he blessed them was not clear, for he lowered his voice. However, after a minute or two it was quite plain that he urged them to a certain course, for he flung his right hand out like an emperor ordering armies, and his chin went up so imperiously high that he moonlight sheened on his fierce eyes.

The hooded figures vanished. They had come from different directions, but as far as one could judge in the uncertain light they were headed one way in single file when they disappeared into the cactus.

"—!" Jim muttered suddenly, and Narayan Singh crept close again.

"Yes, *sahib*? What is it?"

"Can't you see? The *iblis* has gone too—and the wrong way for us, durn him!—toward the moon—due east. If we chase him now he'll simply run."

"I can stalk him, *sahib*. He will never see me."

"No. The others are coming straight along the ridge in the shadows."

"We can do better than that. Catesby?"

Once again you might have laid a handkerchief on all three heads.

"They're coming one by one. Bag the last one alive. Narayan Singh, gag him; take Suliman's turban—have it ready in your hand. I'll pin his arms and get his knife away. I'll whistle to startle him, and then all three of us spring together, downing him at once in the shadow where his friends can't see."

They stowed Suliman in a hollow just over the shoulder of the hill, and crawled into position where a foot-track passed between an anthill and a big cactus in a shallow, spoon-shaped depression of the hilltop. They had hardly hidden themselves when the first man came swinging along at a sort of dog-trot, the pace common to most savage and nearly savage people bent on adventure. He passed so close that they might have touched him, and the reek of cotton clothing soaked in oil was unmistakable.

Six men passed, all going at the same pace, all smelling strongly of the same rancid unguent, with about ten yards between each, dog-trotting to the night's work and in no particular concern just yet to conceal themselves. The seventh man lagged a little, being heavier than the rest and not so free-breathing.

As he drew abreast of them Jim whistled. But instead of checking his pace to look about him the man sprang into the air like a shot buck, and landed in his stride intent on sprinting.

Jim, Catesby and Narayan Singh all sprang at the same instant, and crashed their heads together. But for Catesby's Rugby football days they would have missed their man; but instinct, born of following the ball though a whole pack pounce on him, sent Catesby's right arm shooting out of the scrimmage. Groping wildly at the air, he caught the Arab's ankle. It was greased, but the check before the Arab freed it tripped him, and before he could recover balance all three captors were on top of him, crashing together into the cactus bush.

The Arab could not yell with agony, because Narayan Singh's steely wrist clapped on the cotton gag and held it in place, come life come judgment day. And the Sikh, being topmost, got fewest of the cactus stabs, so swore least. Catesby, underneath, with his arms about the fellow's legs, cursed like a wet cat, hissing canteen blasphemy between his teeth; and Jim, side by side with the prisoner in a bed of inch-long thorns, kept at his task in panting speechlessness that was just as eloquent. There are few points that hurt more acutely than those of a Holy Land cactus.

Jim got the fellow's knife at last, and dropped it in the murderous mess of pikes they fought among. But to hold his arms was another matter. The Arab was greased from head to foot, and his clothes, which might otherwise have served to hold him by were rotten with the oil, tearing whenever they were seized. As the clothing came away from him in rags his naked skin slipped from the grasp more readily than ever; and he was stronger than a bear—sinewy and lithe and, for all his weight, able to wriggle any section of himself that wasn't pegged down tight.

Three or four times he seemed about to slip away from them, struggling like an eel. But Narayan Singh's knee in his stomach combined with the unyielding gag to rob him of breath, so that at last they all rolled out into the open and Jim gasped out a request to Catesby to take his girdle off and bind the fellow's hands and feet.

Catesby was only in the nick of time at that. Struggling to his knees, he was aware of something flashing brightly in the moonlight from behind the ruined cactus bush. He sprang into the shadow and caught Suliman's kukri in the act of descending on the Arab's undefended neck, whirled in both hands like an ax by the eight-year-old. He threw Suliman into the cactus to whimper and recover rectitude.

Then when they had trussed their prisoner and had picked most of the thorns out of him they sat and operated on themselves by moonlight, using pocket-knives and fingernails and hard words, giving the Arab time to get his breath and think up some lies to tell them presently.

It was no use trying to pretend they themselves were Arabs any longer, for they had sworn too lustily in English, to say nothing of Jim's instructions anent the girdle, and Narayan Singh's hoarse imprecations in another tongue.

"Perhaps it's as well," laughed Jim. "Here, Catesby, be a good chap and dig this thorn out from behind my knee. He'll be so puzzled that perhaps he'll lie less, if we can get him to say anything at all. Where's Suliman?"

"I am here. I look for the kukri. It was not the act of a true *khawaja* (gentleman) to throw me in that cactus bush. If you are my *mutahid* (partner), Jimgrim, you will see that I have full vengeance!"

"I'll avenge you. Wait and see. Let's ask the prisoner what he thinks about it. Have you found the kukri?"

Suliman flourished it in the moonlight. Jim stooped over the prisoner and lifted him into a sitting attitude; at sight of the kukri whirling near his head he ducked and fell over again sidewise; for his hands were tied under his knees and one can't keep balance as well as struggle in that position. Jim lifted him again.

"Now," he said in Arabic, "this child vows you are an *iblis*; and he has sworn by the beard of the Prophet to kill the first *iblis* that he sees. We are his friends, here to help him do it. What do you say to that?"

"You have caught the wrong one. I am no *iblis*."

"You fight like one, and you smell worse than one. What then are you?"

"I am a thief."

The man threw such pride into the assertion that Catesby and Narayan Singh both laughed. But Jim was too intent on something else. He shifted his own position so that the moonlight shore directly in the man's face—then nodded.

"Look at me carefully, Mahommed ben Hamza. Do you know me?"

"Jimgrim! *Ilhamdilla!* (Thank God!) Now I am all right."

"No, you're not, you scoundrel!"

"Man without virtue I may be, since Jimgrim says it, who knows so much; but not for nothing did I help thee at El-Kerak, when a word from me would have ended thy career. I say I am all right. *Ilhamdilla!*"

"You think I'm easy," Jim answered, "but I tell you my friends here are ruthless."

"Then you and I will fight them. I am not afraid."

"What brought you from thieving in the Hebron *suk* (market)?"

"What were you doing yonder?"

Jim pointed to the hill two hundred yards away on which the leper had danced.

"What but obtaining magic against bullet and bayonet? What else could a dervish do for me? However, he forgot to bless me for ambushment by the way, or even you, Jimgrim, would not have been clever or strong enough to take me, with twice as many men."

"Then you think his dance is efficacious?"

"Surely. All the thieves go to him, and how many get caught? A very few get shot, and a very few get stabbed, but those are the ones who scoffed at him. He is a driver of hard bargains, but his magic works."

"Hard bargains, eh?"

"Leper's bargains. A man must leave two-thirds of all he steals, or the equivalent at a place appointed, or suffer the curse. None dares fail him."

"I drive still harder bargains," Jim answered.

"Aye, and keep them. Loose my bonds, Jimgrim; thou and I are old friends."

"Not so fast. Are your wife and child at Hebron, Mahommed ben Hamza?"

"Unless ill luck overtook them between yesterday and now."

"And you still own the little vineyard—that profitable little vineyard beside the Jerusalem Road?"

"Surely. That was my father's legacy to me, his firstborn."

"And the stone house in the Haret el-Akkabi (the quarter of the makers of goatskin water-bags)—does that belong to you still?"

"Aye."

"Since I have caught you red-handed on your way to steal from Ludd Camp, and you have confessed in front of witnesses, do you not see I am in position to drive a very hard bargain?"

"Between friends?"

"Between a thief and one who can get that thief fined so heavily that there would be no more orchard paying profits on the Jerusalem Road, and no more home in the Haret el-Akkabi to bequeath to an only son."

"You would not do that, Jimgrim!"

"I spoke of a bargain."

"Well?"

"Where is that leper to be found by daylight?"

"None knows. None dares inquire."

"Where is the place appointed for his share of the plunder to be left?"

"It is never twice the same."

"Where have you been told to leave two-thirds of what you proposed to steal tonight?"

"Ah-h-h!"

"My friend the Governor of Hebron keeps a nice, clean jail, it is true," said Jim. "And my friend Moustapha Aziz the auctioneer obtains good prices, too. There might be a little something left to you after the fine is paid."

"Jimgrim, if I though you were a liar I would take my chance. The court would never fine me all that much, for since the Turks left there is a law like mother's milk. But you are such a devil that I think you could arrange it. I suppose you know of other charges you could lay against me, and who shall stand against your persistence? Moreover, you are my friend."

"Answer my question then."

"I cannot describe the place."

"Is it near here?"

"Yes."

"Then lead us to it."

"Jimgrim, I am afraid. That dervish who has no name is a capable fellow. He can curse!"

"And I, who hold you prisoner, know all about your property. Which is the lesser evil—a curse that might miss—"

"*Inshalla!*"

"Or my flat promise to get after you in Hebron?"

Mahommed ben Hamza smiled as winningly as a child with a cause to plead.

"You I know of old, Jimgrim. The dervish is new and talks a lot, but his talking did not save me from being caught tonight. Besides, you are my friend. I will lead you to the place."

"Loose his feet, Narayan Singh. Then tie his hands behind his back."

"Nay, Jimgrim! Have I questioned your word once, or lied to you once? Did I lie to you at El-Kerak, when at a word from me they would have thrown you from the castle roof?"

Jim hesitated. He did not want to be hampered by a prisoner on his hands that night, yet he would have had to return to camp in order to lock him up. But on the other hand he did not want the responsibility of letting him go. The best plan seemed to be to make a stipulation with definite limits, which the man would probably observe implicitly and then vamoose.

"Just what do you promise?" he asked.

"I will lead you to the place where the dervish told us we must leave his *bakshish*."

"All right. Swear to it."

"By the holy mosque of El-Kalil—by the tomb of my father, on whom be blessings—by the—"

"That will do. Loose him, Narayan Singh—but keep a close eye on him."

"*Mashallah!* I could not run if I were minded," laughed Mahommed ben Hamza, stretching himself. "I would rather a camel knelt on my belly another time than that fellow of yours who gagged me. This way, your honors."

* * * *

He led them along the ridge toward the spot where the leper had danced, so brightly and at such an angle that whoever was abroad could hardly have helped seeing them the moment they should desert the scant cover of the scrub. Mahommed ben Hamza did not care; his own need of secrecy was at an end for that night, and his part of the bargain was to show the way; he deliberately chose the open path until Jim called a halt, midway along the ridge.

There he left Catesby and Narayan Singh, bidding Suliman mark the place carefully.

"Now down on your belly and crawl!" he ordered. "And if you make a noise or show yourself you shall surely wish I was only a camel; I'll land on top of you like a troop of cavalry! You, too, Suliman—crawl!"

On hands and knees, picking out the shadows of the cactus and taking their chance of snake, centipedes and scorpions, they crept up to the spot where the leper had danced, and Jim went aside to examine it, wondering what sort of hollow his pirouetting must have scooped out of the sand. But in place of a hole was an ancient Moslem tombstone long since fallen flat, and now worn smooth in the middle where the man's feet had rubbed it night after night.

"Come away, Jimgrim; the place is bewitched!" Mahommed ben Hamza whispered.

But Jim was not satisfied until he had worked his fingers under the stone and lifted it to see what might be underneath. For the next three minutes he was busy killing about a dozen of the little deadly vipers that infest the plains of Palestine, using the kukri snatched from Suliman's hand.

"What did I tell you?" grumbled Mahommed ben Hamza. "Did not I say it is bewitched?"

After that they crawled downhill, scouting extremely carefully because the moon shone on a smooth surface of sand where cactus and shadow were scant. At the foot of the long slope was a winding nullah, and there, because of the shadow, they dared stand upright. Mahommed ben Hamza led along it to a sandy amphitheater a quarter of a mile away, and stopped in front of one of those open tombs with which all Palestine abounds.

"There, that is the place."

"Inside or outside?"

"We were to lay the loot inside."

"Go in and see if the leper is in there now."

"Allah forbid! Besides, Jimgrim, my bargain is finished. I was to lead to the place, that is all."

"True."

"Having kept my promise I am now free."

"Gee, that was foolish of me! I ordered Narayan Singh to keep an eye on you, and then left him behind."

"So now I go. Good-by, Jimgrim. Don't shoot, for the dervish might hear—and besides you are my friend!"

"But if I catch you away from Hebron before I visit the place," Jim answered, "you shall wish I had shot you, do you understand? After all, I think—perhaps—"

He drew his automatic and cocked it very deliberately; but Mahommed ben Hamza was out of sight among the shadows almost before the spring of the pistol clicked.

CHAPTER V

"Aye, father of reprimands, but where?"

Catesby and Narayan Singh waited interminably, watching the moon mount overhead and passing from mere impatient to restlessness to anxiety as more than an hour went by without any sign of Jim. Officer and enlisted man, Englishman and Sikh, they naturally kept their distance, each respecting the other's prejudices; and they lay low for fear of scouting desert thieves. Once they heard a shot ring out somewhere in the direction of the camp, but that was nothing unusual since thieve had become so busy.

At last Narayan Singh crawled close to Catesby and with an upward jerk of his thumb toward the moon began to speak in that low voice which is so hugely better than a whisper.

"*Sahib*, I have orders to bring our Jimgrim back to Jerusalem alive!"

"What do you propose, Narayan Singh?"

"My orders to take care of him was from my own colonel, *sahib*. It is good to obey."

"We'll give him ten more minutes. If he doesn't come then or send the boy for us we'll try to find him."

"Good."

Narayan Singh spent most of the ten minutes examining his pistol and a long, keen knife that he carried under his tunic, arranging both so that he could reach them instantly with either hand. But there remained ninety interminable seconds.

"Let me see your pistol, *sahib*. I have known these automatics to jam. Sand in the fodder kills mules and horses, but I have seen officers die more quickly for lack of a man to detect sand in their pistol locks."

Catesby laughed and handed the weapon over. It is only the raw subaltern who is too proud to be nursed by a war-wise enlisted man. Aware that his weapon was spotless clean, he was too wise to discourage the Sikh's thoughtfulness.

"Now are the ten minutes not up?"

"Thirty seconds," said Catesby, glancing at his wristwatch. "Pistol all right?"

"A little heavy on the pull. Is it a new one?"

"Yes."

"Then take care to aim to the left, *sahib*, if it has to be used in a hurry. Now—?"

"Yes, come on."

Catesby led, but only for the sake of form. Narayan Singh's low voice from just behind did all the counseling.

"Jimgrim went first to the place where the *shaitan* (devil) danced. I saw him."

The shadows were shorter now, and it was not so easy to keep cover and make rapid progress. On the hilltop they abandoned all effort to conceal themselves. Catesby stooped to examine the tombstone, and discovered some of the snakes that Jim had killed with the kukri. But Narayan Singh had seen them first.

"Beware, *sahib*! A snake dies slowly; cut in halves they can bite yet for an hour or two."

He fidgeted until Catesby came away from them.

Now the moon proved friend as well as enemy, for the Sikh's keen eyes picked up the trail Mahommed ben Hamza made in the sand, crossed once in a while by those of Jim and Suliman hurrying from bush to bush. But at the bottom of the long slope where the footsteps turned into the narrow *wady* they were confused by those of six or seven more men hurrying in single file in the same direction. In the one spot where the moonlight shone on the bed of the *wady* Narayan Singh stooped and scooped up a handful of earth. It was sticky. He beckoned Catesby into a hollow on one side of the track.

"Strike a match, *sahib*. Carefully! A match can be seen for miles. Thus—ah—blood it is, and almost warm—scarcely begun to harden."

They both examined every inch of the ground for ten or fifteen yards.

"There was no fight in this place. Whoever bled got his punishment elsewhere. Perhaps they carried a wounded man—who can tell in this dim light? See—there is blood again, *sahib*. Shall we follow?"

There was nothing else they could do in the circumstances. It was surely contrary to all the rules of warfare, civilized or guerilla, for two men in the dark to stalk seven down a narrow, winding *wady*, around any turn of which the seven might wait and pounce on them.

But Catesby was no whit behind Narayan Singh in eagerness to serve his friend; and to turn back was unthinkable, for instance, as to let the Sikh go first into danger, even if his were the keenest eyes. There are prerogatives that no man willingly relinquishes. Catesby strode forward.

* * * *

Fifty-four paces down the *wady*, by his own count, he tripped and nearly fell over an Arab corpse.

For a minute they took cover near the corpse and listened. Then Narayan Singh knelt beside it and his long, brown fingers searched swiftly. Someone had covered up the face with the head-dress and bound the covering fast. He tugged it off.

"God be praised, it is not Jimgrim!" he growled. "The body is quite warm—not dead ten minutes."

His fingers searched inside the clothes and presently found the "emergency exit" through which the man's life had fled.

"He died by a bayonet, *sahib*. Come and feel. There is no mistaking that wound. Likely a Sikh did it, for the thrust forced the middle rib apart and broke the lower one. These were camp-thieves returning from the night's work, and one got more than he bargained for."

The fingers searched again, feeling skillfully for anything of value; but the man's friends had taken that precaution first, and even the usual amulets and necklace of prayer-beads were missing. However, the father East a man is born the more meticulously detailed is his genius for looting (so that the Punjaubi and the Jew from Bokhara can thrive where the Arab starves, the Chinaman can fatten on what they leave, and the Japanese out-thieves them all).

Presently the Sikh covered the dead man's face again and waited for Catesby to lead on, but the Englishman hesitated. Thieves (supposing that they were thieves) who took such trouble to cover up a dead man's face were hardly likely to leave the body long at the mercy of jackals and hyenas.

There was apparently only one possible way they could take returning. They might send two men back for the body, or return in force. He might leave Narayan Singh in hiding there to watch, and scout forward alone. Narayan Singh could deal alone with two or three men; but six or seven would overwhelm him.

Finally he adopted the inevitable British compromise and, beckoning the Sikh to follow him, turned back a little way to avoid making more footprints on the sand. At the first place where the bank of the *wady* sloped fairly easily he began to climb it and discovered, as he expected, easy enough going at the top.

"Now, Narayan Singh, we'll scout along together as far as the last point from which we can overlook the *wady*. There I'll leave you and carry on. If I need you I'll fire my pistol. If you need me, do the same.

"You won't be able to see down into the *wady*, but if anybody comes along it you can hear; in that case scout closer. Shoot to kill if you want to, but mind you don't shoot Jimgrim *sahib* by mistake!"

The Sikh's disgust and disappointment were as plain as if he had dared voice them. A hound would have submitted as cheerfully. He approved neither of dividing forces nor of squandering his own trained senses on any passive form of usefulness.

"Forward, *sahib!*" he urged; and the tone of his voice bordered on insolence. "Shall Jimgrim and the *butcha* need us and we play vulture above a carcass?"

Catesby laughed dryly.

"Do as I say," he ordered.

They were able to go quite a long way without losing sight of the black, velvet-looking belt of gloom that was the *wady* bottom, and Catesby's plan proved not so contemptible after all. Keeping a company of Sikhs in fighting trim for months past had given him a knowledge of all that countryside that could not desert him in the dark, and presently they reached a low eminence from which they could look down into the *wady* in either direction.

By that time, too, the moon shone at such an angle that the darkness below them was considerably broken up and patches of sand were beginning to be visible in places. To their left, clearly outlined in the yellow light, lay a sandy amphitheater, and if they had only known it they could see the opening of the tomb to which the Arab had led Jim and Suliman.

Nevertheless they seemed to have missed their opportunity, and Narayan Singh suddenly swore a streak of Indian oaths that would have made a mere comminating prelate shudder with mixed envy and dread. Down below them, passing in single file across a yellow sand-patch to their right, they caught sight of men's figures moving swiftly. Catesby counted five, the Sikh six, but there might have been more because of the shadows, and some might have crossed the patch of light before they saw the others. They were all swallowed in black night again before the brain could get any clear impression of their general appearance.

Catesby made up his mind swiftly enough then, and Narayan Singh approved, since decision entailed action.

"Come on! After them from the rear!"

They slid down the sandbank into the *wady* and started to run, keeping in the middle where the track was loose and soft, so as to make less noise. Neither man knew exactly what they meant to do other than force the party ahead to stand and give an account of themselves. If that should entail a free fight, well and good; the Sikh, at least, would sooner fight than not, and Catesby had no objection.

But the one paramount, essential objective was to get tidings of Jim Grim, and neither of them made a single stipulation as to ways of means. They simply ran.

Whether or not they were gaining on their quarry they never knew; for suddenly, down the sandbank just abreast of them, panting, staggering, tripping, tottering, tumbling into their arms to sob and cling to them—Suliman came like a bolt out of the night—too scared and breathless to explain himself, kicking and punching at Narayan Singh because he should comprehend without words—too bewildered to speak English to Catesby, who had scant Arabic.

Catesby was not much of a hand with children. He tried sternness to antidote hysteria, and succeeded only in making his victim cry. So Narayan Singh squatted in the *wady* as if time were no consideration, and took the boy in his lap.

"A brave fellow!" he said. "Truly a brave fellow! Out in the night alone and not afraid of leopards! A soldier in the making! A swift runner! A man of deeds, not words! A scout who knows friends in the dark and can find them! A skirmisher who takes a cliff-side like a warhorse galloping! Truly a proper friend for such a one as Jimgrim! And what said Jimgrim? I wager had had a message for Narayan Singh?"

"Curse you religion! Curse your mother and her family! What are you waiting for? Let me go!"

The youngster struggled, and struck the Sikh's face with his fists, but stirred no reprisals. Narayan Singh held on an laughed.

"Aha! A ruffian! A fighting man! A very Rustum (a famous warrior) at the age of eight. I wager Jimgrim sent him out to fight the *iblis!*"

The word *iblis* loosened the floods of speech at last. Suliman spat into the Sikh's black beard and followed up the illustration with his text.

"Come and get him! Come quick! The *iblis* sits and spits at him! Jimgrim is bewitched. The *iblis* curses him. Jimgrim's pistol is bewitched; he can't use it. The *iblis* laughs. I ran to find you and you were gone, so I came back to kill the *iblis* with my kukri. Now you sit and grin, you son of sixty dogs, while the iblis murders Jimgrim. Have you no heart? Have you no courage? Jimgrim is in danger!"

"Aye, father of reprimands! But where?"

"Where? In the cave, of course! In the cave, idiot!"

"Which cave, O father of whirlwinds?"

"Which cave, Narayan Singh? As if there were more than one! Can Jimgrim be in two caves?"

"Can you lead us to the cave?"

"No! I have lost my way!"

That admission was altogether too much for Catesby, who was listening in shadow. He stepped closer to try again what stern authority might do. But Narayan Singh waved him back with an imploring gesture, and resumed the milder method.

"Such a scout! Such a father of long memories! I wager he has not forgotten what I taught him in Jerusalem. You were in the cave, Suliman? And you came out of the cave? Then on which side shone the moon—on this or that hand? This hand I wager. No? That one? Ah! And you crossed this *wady* to reach the place where I waited with the *sahib*? Ah! Then the cave is this way. Come!"

He got up, took the child by the hand and led him along the *wady* in the opposite direction to that in which they had been running, Catesby following in agonies of impatience. At every projection Narayan Singh would stop and try to get the boy to recognize it, but it was not until they reached the open amphitheater that Suliman gave a gasp of sheer excitement and began to run.

"There! There is the cave! I see it! Hurry, Narayan Singh! Curse you for a crawling beetle! Pick me up and carry me, I am *halas*—finish!"

Narayan Singh gathered him up in his hairy arms, gentle as a woman's, but as strong as two pythons, and broke into a double. The moonlight shone straight into the cave mouth, and Catesby, having no load, reached it first. By the time Narayan Singh overtook him and had set down Suliman, Catesby was disappearing head first into a black hole, sending his voice ahead of him:

"Grim! Hullo! Jim Grim! Hullo, Uncle Sam, are you there? The reserves are coming, Grim—hold on!"

Suliman was next into the hole, charging under the Sikh's legs and pulling out his kukri as he scrambled, yelling too:

"Oh Jimgrim! *Taib* (all right) Jimgrim! All right, Jimgrim! Coming! We are here!"

They plunged forward into utter darkness; and because Suliman was to busy shouting to think of warning them about the tricks of the place they all three took a header down a four-foot drop into the echoing home of blackness.

Narayan Singh proved heavy, for it is bone and thew that weigh, not fat. It took Catesby two minutes to recover breath, and then at last he struck a match. He held it high over his head, and the light showed all four walls of a cavern.

"Grim! Where are you?"

The cavern, with a row of sepulchers hewn into the walls, was empty. The echoes mocked them. Catesby struck match after match, and they peered together into every niche and cranny, finding nothing but a dollop of candle-grease to prove that anyone had ever been in there.

Catesby burned his fingers with his last match, and the blackness of the womb of darkness shut them in again.

"Too late? Surely not too late?" muttered Narayan Singh.

Then Suliman lifted up his voice and yelled:

"He is gone! Oh, Jimgrim! Prince of men! That *iblis* has eaten him! Curse the *iblis*! Curse his religion and his mother and his eyes and his belly and his teeth! In the name of Allah, may his soul be flung into the fire that burns. May devils torture him forever. Oh, my Jimgrim! Oh-oh—ai-ee-ee!"

He flung himself face down and beat the floor of the cavern with his fists, sobbing his heart out for his vanished hero.

CHAPTER VI

"Thieves again!"

The worst part of scheming for your own advancement is that sooner of later, and generally sooner, you are forced to employ paid assistance; and in the very nature of things such men as will assist are all self-seekers on their own account. The only safe ambition for even the cleverest men is on behalf of an ideal.

There are plenty of instances. Napoleon obsessed with the thought of lifting France out of the ruck of misery and restoring his country to her right place in the sun was invincible. Napoleon on a throne, scheming to make himself an ancestor of kings, was only dangerous. And Brigadier-General Jenkins was an immeasurable way behind Napoleon, without ever having possessed high ideals of any kind, although he could talk about them in a florid way that deceived some folk.

At about the time when Jim left camp on the trail of the *iblis* Jenkins was burning overtime oil in the wooden shack that did duty for office, with a corner of one window left uncovered in order that the world might appreciate his devotion to duty.

But he had given up sitting at the desk and rummaging through papers. Papers were the bane of his existence. Covering it under an air of lordly military scorn for trifles, he had been afflicted all his life with carelessness at odd moments, such as would account, for instance, for the R.T.O.'s confidence in washing his hands of the stolen TNT. Jenkins had received a memorandum about that explosive and mislaid it; now he had lost another paper, and this time there was no one else on whom he dared lay blame.

If it had been an official document he could certainly have pounced his clerk, but unfortunately it was something about which it was to be hoped the clerk knew nothing. If the clerk did know, then the sooner that unfortunate should leave for far-off parts the better. The worst of it was that he was expecting a visit that evening from the man who had signed the paper, and he had reasons for needing it to flourish under that individual's nose.

He paced up and down the narrow office, casting huge shadows that made his mustache seem like a tea-pot handle and annoyed him, for he was vain of personal appearance as of everything else. Every now and then he paused to rap his forehead with a clenched fist, as if to shake into action that magnificent memory of which he boasted. Then the pacing was resumed, while his lower lip sucked at the corner of the red mustache to present the offending shadow.

One incident kept recurring to mind that he hoped explained the loss away, but he would have given a month's pay to be sure of it. He remembered a soiled, creased, dog-eared hundred-piaster note that had come in halves and had to be stuck together. He had sat at his desk—he remembered that distinctly—clipped a strip of paper with the shears, gummed the strip and joined the two halves of the note.

In all likelihood he had crumpled up the remainder of the piece of paper and thrown it into the box that did duty for wastebasket, but of that he could not be certain. It was possible that was the missing document. And he could not for the life of him remember to whom of for what purpose he had paid out the banknote, repaired with a strip of paper that might have Arabic handwriting on it.

He might have paid a mess-bill with it, or settled a bridge account—although he very rarely lost at cards—in which case the note was probably long ago in circulation far enough away to be out of danger. That was to be hoped, but hope is often a fidgety weakling.

An incident nagged his memory. He had paid one hundred piasters on a recent occasion to the man who was coming to see him tonight—the very man under whose nose he wanted to brandish the lost signature.

As he turned for another worried beat up and down the room a Sikh sentry rapped on the door to announce his visitor. He went behind the desk and studied his appearance in the little canteen store looking-glass for a minute before answering, twisting his mustache straight and practicing a couple of grimaces. He believed as thoroughly in advertisement as any manufacturer of patent pills, and never overlooked the cover of the capsule.

* * * *

For an Arab the visitor seemed overconfident. He was a little man, dressed in expensive European clothes, but with a *tarboosh* at least a size too small for him so that it sat jauntily on a head that grew very suddenly narrow above the ears; and like many little men he walked mincingly, suggesting an insect—but an insect with a sting, for his smile did not succeed in hiding malice. He was the sort of man one would instinctively keep at a distance. But his voice was like oil on troubled waters.

"I have nothing but good news for your honor," he began, smiling jubilantly. "I confess myself more than ever amazed at your genius that suggested this plan to organize Arab thieves and blame their thefts on the Zionists. It works! Never was such a thieving—tee-hee-hee! And a fair proportion of the plunder is already stowed in a place owned by the Zionist Committee—hee-hee!—such a joke!—isn't it exquisite?"

"Sit down! And listen to me, Charkas. How many times have I to tell you that I've nothing to do with your plans? I won't have you as much as suggest it, even in private. Do you understand me?"

Ibrahim Charkas folded one hand on the other, chose the edge of an uncomfortable chair and sat down facing him. The corners of his mouth looked meek, and his eyes immensely mischievous.

"I'm willing to help you Arabs, *sub rosa*, so to speak. And I'm willing that it should be known in the right quarter at the right time that I have been your friend all along. But nothing indiscreet—you understand me?"

"Certainly. Yes, indeed. And when the time comes you may rest assured we shall show ourselves most grateful—practically grateful."

"Um-m-m! By the way Charkas, do you remember a hundred-piaster note I gave you the other day for expenses? There was a hundred, and I think four fifties and ten tens."

"Yes, indeed. You have been most generous. I was wondering tonight whether I might not ask—"

"D'you happen to have that hundred by you?"

"I have a hundred piasters—"

"I mean the original bank-note that I gave you."

"No, sir. Why?"

"I suspect it's a bad one. I'd like to give you another for it."

"Tee-hee-hee! You need not worry, general. It has been passed on long ago. Whoever has it now may do the worrying. Hee-hee! But I would like some more money for expenses."

"Damn it! D'you take me for a millionaire?"

"No, sir. Indeed I know better. But these agitators all need wages, and if we are to work up a proper feeling against the Zionists there must be plenty of paid men at work."

"Haven't you Arabs any guts, that you can't raise a campaign fund among you?"

"Ah-h-h! We are mostly poor, and those who are not are inclined to keep out of trouble. My own little business in the *suk* (bazaar) is not profitable nowadays, because the soldiers buy all they require in the canteen at prices I cannot meet. Now if I had a few hundred piasters tonight—"

"Sorry, Charkas; I've no cash by me."

"But a check, general? A check made out to bearer—"

"What do you take me for? How many times must I repeat that my name doesn't appear in connection with this business? Besides, I'm getting sick of it. It's time to bring things to a head. Major Grim has been sent down from Jerusalem to inquire into the thieving, and he's one of those persistent men who generally get what they're after. The way to make the most of that is to let him discover the loot as soon as possible in the hands of Zionists, and then advertise it here, in Egypt, and in England."

"Tee-hee-hee! Exquisite! As I said, a fair proportion of the loot is already—"

"I don't want to know where it is. Don't tell me. News reached me by mail this morning that the feeling at the Foreign Office is turning strongly against the Zionists at present. The fools have been demanding too much, with the result that pro-Arab sentiment is gaining ground. Much the same story comes from Egypt.

Anything just now that puts the Zionists in a more unfavorable light would be opportune. You may depend on it, Major Grim will run that loot to ground in short order, so you'd better cover up your own tracks."

"Oh, my tracks are very well covered."

There was a suggestion of insolence underlying the certainty in the Arab's voice that made Jenkins turn suddenly and face him.

"How d'ye mean?"

"You are powerful. I look to you for protection in case of necessity. Otherwise—"

"Look here! Are you fooling yourself by any chance? Do you suppose I'd budge one inch to protect you? You people have no sense of proportion. To help the Arab cause—*sub rosa* as I said— is one thing; to ruin my whole career by becoming involved in your intrigues is another, and doesn't appeal to me at all. I'd let you hang rather than lift a finger."

He glared at Charkas with dark eyes that had cowed many a subordinate and rescued him in many an awkward moment. He had made a deliberate study of that frown and the attitude that went with it, growing expert in their use but rather overestimating their value on the strength of occasional successes.

The Arab flinched like an animal under the lash. Jenkins turned his back on him. It was more from habit than intention that he strode behind the desk and faced the looking-glass.

Ibrahim Charkas was less cowed that he chose to seem, being one of those men who can keep their wits alert under a protecting mask of physical fear. The moment Jenkins' back was turned he leaned toward the desk and began searching the papers that lay scattered all over it in the confusion made by Jenkins himself half an hour previously. His fingers were as swift and supple as a card-shaper's, and his eyes, glancing every second at Jenkins' back, as wary as a rat's.

In less than thirty seconds he had spotted a railway notice of consignments due to arrive. Watching his chance, he flipped it toward the corner of the desk. A second more and he had it in his pocket. Then Jenkins turned on him.

"Give that back!"

"Give what back?"

"Don't try to argue. I watched you in the glass. Give it here. It's in that pocket. Out with it!"

With his head sunk between his shoulders, feet apart, ready to jump for his life, and his eyes looking like black shoe-buttons, the Arab laid the paper on the desk. Jenkins glanced at it.

"So-ho! So that's the way of it! Done it before half a dozen times no doubt! That's how they knew about the TNT, eh? You stole the memorandum off my desk. I remember now, you were in here that morning. What else have you taken?"

"Nothing else, sir."

"I mean on other occasions."

"Nothing. I am no thief. I did not take any memorandum. As for this, it was unintentional—mere nervousness—I did it without thinking—I—"

"Oh, piffle! Sit where you are. Now—look up at me. You've been in here to my knowledge twice since the morning that TNT memorandum came.

"On the second occasion you followed up a letter you had written me. You said you had information too important to be put in writing. But you put a lot in that letter, didn't you? It was pretty compromising, wasn't it? And the additional information turned out to be so insignificant that I wondered why you bothered to come.

"I know now. I was looking for that letter tonight, and it's missing. It lay in this top drawer. You stole it back—now didn't you?"

Jenkins fairly yelled the last words at him and Charkas nearly shrank out of his skin.

"I did not! On my honor, I swear I did not!"

Jenkins reached for a whalebone riding-whip that hung from a nail on the wall.

"Admit it, you bastard, or I'll thrash the life out of you."

To Jenkins' surprise, instead of capitulating and confessing the Arab grew suddenly calm.

"Why should I confess to what I did not do?" he answered. "It is you who should be ashamed not I. If you have lost that letter you have betrayed me faithlessly, because anyone who finds it can make use of it to ruin me. If that is so, I hope it will ruin you too.

"It was addressed to you. Your name was on it. If I am arrested I shall denounce you. You would better let me get away from here. Give me some money and I will go to Egypt."

Jenkins laughed. But he returned the whip to its nail on the wall, recovering his temper with an effort.

"I know what happened to the letter," he said. "I tore it up the other day. I was testing you. Seeing you take that paper just now in your—ah—fit of nervousness, I naturally jumped to conclusions and suspected you of other thefts. That's an old trick, you know, to startle an man into confessing something he did do by accusing him of doing something you know he didn't. You stood the test, Charkas.

"You'd better go now, though—it's inviting suspicion to be found talking with you in here so late at night. Don't forget—Major Grim is already on the job; so cover up your tracks, and be ready to accuse the Zionists. Good night."

"You gave me a severe shock to my nervous system, but—good night, sir."

Jenkins whistled the sentry and gave him orders to escort the Arab to the gate. Then he blew out the lamp, locked the door, and went to his own tent, where he sat for a few minutes humming to himself.

"So he stole that TNT memorandum, did he? I wonder if he took that letter too, or whether I destroyed it by accident. Um-m-m! So he thinks he can ruin me, does he? He's a mean little rat, and he might make trouble.

"Pity I accused Catesby, but that can't be helped now. I shall have to get Charkas on some other count—he's best out of the way. Um-m-m! Hullo, what's that!"

A rifle shot spat out through the darkness near at hand, and was followed by a deal of shouting.

"Thieves again!" yelled a subaltern's voice, and there was a rush of officers from the mess marquee to lend a hand in the hunt.

Jenkins buttoned up his tunic, buckled on his belt, and hurried after them to add to his laurels by being officious even if he reached the scene too late.

Those night raids take place swiftly, and when discovered the thieves don't wait to be surrounded. He arrived in time to receive the report from three subalterns, all speaking together breathlessly.

"Two of our Sikhs wounded, sir, but one of them swears he got home with his bayonet first. There's blood on the bayonet to prove it. The thieves got away with their dead man, and three rifles and some other stuff that they'd snaffled before they were seen. That's all, sir."

"Quite enough, too," snapped Jenkins. "It's a disgraceful business. I shall have an inquiry at once, and fix the blame. Perfectly disgraceful!"

He himself passed on the report to General Anthony, who came hurrying up a moment later, followed by his aide.

"I've been giving these rifle raids a lot of thought and close attention," he added in conclusion. "It's my belief that when the facts are out you'll find Zionists are at the bottom of it all."

Anthony looked hard at him in the light of a sentry's lantern.

"Anyone who could prove that would be entitled to great credit," he said slowly. "Have you seen that the wounded Sikhs have attention? No, never mind; I'll go myself."

CHAPTER VII

"I can deal with twenty-five as easily as one!"

It was Jim's intention, once he had found the leper's rendez-vous and got rid of the rather embarrassing company of Mahom-med ben Hamza, to return for Catesby and Narayan Singh, or perhaps to send Suliman for them if the boy could be induced to go alone.

But there was something about the dark, open mouth of that tomb that fixed his attention for the moment. It did not differ particularly from a thousand others dotted here and there within a radius of a few miles; there was a sort of porch, perhaps a dozen feet deep, roughly hewn out of the hillside without any significant figures; and down in a corner of that was a dark hole of not more than half a man's height, leading no doubt into a natural cave beyond.

But while he looked, wondering what attracted him, a distinct sound emerged from the hole. Noises in the night, propelled from a cave by the echoing walls, are not easy to recognize; but if it sounded like anything familiar it was a human hiccough.

Any of a number of creatures might have made the noise; owls, jackals, hyenas, badgers, rats—for those old tombs, once robbers have plundered them, make the handiest imaginable dens for wild beasts, provided their opening stands above the water-line, as this one did.

They business of being a hunter, whether of animals or men, produced two salient characteristics; a tendency to form opin-ion in advance as to what the hunted will most likely do, and an equally alert ability to throw preformed opinion to the winds at the first hint.

Jim had made up his mind that the leper would hardly risk waiting at the rendezvous, and for several reasons. In the first place the cave was almost certainly a trap, with only one opening. Whoever waited inside it could form no notion of what was passing outside, and would be at the mercy of superior numbers; men who had risked their lives to steal rifles might likely balk at surrendering the booty to one lone individual within the narrow compass of a grave.

To be morally afraid of a dervish dancing like a devil on a hill was one thing; to fear him at all when face to face within four walls would be another. A man with the knowledge of Arab human nature that the leper had displayed would appreciate that certainty.

On the other hand, to wait at a little distance, watch for returning plunderers, perhaps even warn them sternly from an overlooking point of vantage, and come down to collect the booty after they had placed it in the cave and after making sure that the coast was clear, would be safe, circumspect and sane—cynical, in fact, in keeping with the cynicism that made use of the leprosy and religious emotion for unlawful ends.

Jim's first idea consequently was to wait at a point of vantage, too, and descend on the leper in turn and catch him red-handed whenever he should descend to possess the loot.

But there is no accounting for the recklessness of criminals, or the arrogance of men who think that fear gives them a hold over their accomplices. Cunning though he is, and careful though he is in a thousand ways, the charlatan who practices on superstition is once in a while more incautious than a sheep-fed wolf; like the wolf he takes outrageous chances after use has made the game seem simple.

Jim sat down in front of the tomb and listened, while Suliman clung to him in the hysteria of small-boy terror of bogies. For a long time the only movement was Suliman's trembling, and the only sound the footfall of some small night animal borne on an almost imperceptible breeze. But then the cough, or sneeze, or belch, or whatever it was, was repeated and Suliman hid his face in Jim's *abyi* (long-sleeved Arab cloak), shuddering as if he hoped to crawl out of his skin.

"Now," said Jim, "we decide whether or not you wear girl's clothes for a year. I'm going in there. Are you coming too?"

* * * *

It was an awful test of courage for a child of eight, with a shameful alternative. But Jim, whose own youth had been one long adventure with hardship and disadvantage, in which the only penalty he had learned to loathe was self-contempt, was not friend of compromise. Shameful alternatives were things he faced and turned his back on in New England at such an early age that decision had become a habit; and what a man has done repeatedly himself he finds it hard to believe another cannot do. Suliman knew perfectly well from grim experience that Jim would be as good as his word.

"I am a man, not a woman. I will not wear girl's garments. Must I go in first?"

"No; I'll lead."

"Lead on then, Jimgrim."

"Good for you, youngster."

But Jim was minded to test him to the utmost.

"Seeing you're willing, you may stay outside if you like."

"No. I am a man. Lead on."

"All right. But listen; not a word to me in English. Hold your tongue—listen with all your might—and try to take your cue from me. Now are you ready?"

Jim produced a pocket electric torch and, stooping beside the black hole, flashed the light across the opening. Little by little, as nothing happened, he directed the light down into the hole, keeping himself out of the path of possible bullets. But it was a long passage and not straight, high enough inside for a man to stand without stooping and wide enough to carry in a body on a bier, but turning so abruptly after fifteen or twenty feet that there was nothing to be gained by peering in.

The fact that the flashlight had not scared out any animal was possibly presumptive proof that a man was in there who had scared the usual denizens to flight already; but in that case all that he had certainly done so far was to give the man notice of his coming.

So he crouched into the opening and stepped down and forward without further preliminary, flashing the light again and trusting to its glare to spoil the aim of any man or beast disposed to murder. Suliman, forgetting the solace of the kukri, clung to the skirts of his *abyi* and followed breathlessly.

He took the turn in a hurry, for there is nothing to be gained by giving your enemy time to think until you have the weather gage of him so surely that thinking may induce him to surrender. But again nothing happened, and Suliman's teeth were chattering so loudly that Jim could not be sure whether or not he heard something moving in the darkness.

Immediately beyond the turn the passage sloped steeply into a natural cave, with a sheer drop at the end of three or four feet to the cave floor. Somebody might easily be crouching there, so he switched the light off suddenly and took the last lap with a run and a jump, leaving Suliman at the corner, scared out of his wits but grimly silent. The instant his feet touched the floor he faced about and turned on the light again, rather expecting to see the leper rise from beneath the opening and start to scramble away. But again nothing happened, except that Suliman took hold of courage with clenched teeth and came charging down after him, blinded by the torchlight in his eyes and pitching into the cave head foremost, unhurt by a miracle.

The tomb proved to be low, but long and wide—thirty feet at least each way, with a smooth floor showing traces of the chisel, although the roof was in its natural state. A swift examination of the walls by the torchlight showed deep recesses cut into the sides about four feet above the floor, each one doubtless in its day a separate sepulcher. Jim started to examine them one by one, commencing from the nearest to the entrance, and got no farther. His man was there—alive, alert, apparently amused.

Squatting in the mouth of a hole that once held human bones, like an Indian idol, except that most of the Indian gods lack humor, the leper smiled and said nothing, resting his chin in the hollow of one hand and his elbow on one knee, blinking at the light.

He looked abominably leprous. Whole patches of his skin from face to heels were glistening white and scaly. Yet his muscles seemed as firm as a horse's and as magnificently molded underneath the skin, while the expression on his face was not that of a man grown used to gnawing agony or the leprous local anesthesia. His eyes shown healthy in the torchlight, and except for the disgusting state of parts of his skin he looked more like an athlete in condition than a sick man.

For two minutes no one spoke. Then the leper reached behind him with his left hand, and Jim covered him instantly with his pistol.

But all that the groping hand brought forth was a candle-end and a match. The *iblis* set the candle-end on a ledge in the broken wall of the recess and lit it, never moving the rest of his body or shifting the position of his chin. So Jim put out the torch, to save the meager battery.

"Shoot him, Jimgrim," Suliman whispered unable to bear the tension any longer.

"*Sa'id, ya Jimgrim!*" boomed the *iblis*.

Having snatched Jim's name out of the silence as it were, he saw fit to speak. Moreover, having apparently only his sharp wits for a weapon, he proposed to take the upper hand by assuming the role of questioner.

"What manner of name is Jimgrim? What sort of Arab prowls by night with such a name for the *diba* (hyenas) to laugh at?"

The man's voice was pleasant, though his consonants were hard and vowels coarse. Being an Egyptian his opinion on the subject of Arab names was certain to be at fault as well as unimportant. The Arabs themselves gave Jimgrim his name. Jim answered instantly, mocking him in turn.

"Do the lepers of Egypt *all* smear on the sickness form a paint-pot?" he asked.

The *iblis* blinked steadily, still smiling, but saw fir not to answer.

"And smear so clumsily that the pain peels off at the edges here and there?" Jim asked again.

"What kind of cursed mother of impudence brought thee forth?" asked the *iblis*.

"One whose son can smell an Egyptian from half a mile away, and knows the look of paint, O father of unimportant questions," Jim replied.

"Come close. Touch me then, and count how many days until you too have leprosy!" sneered the *iblis*.

Suliman clutched at Jim to hold back, but Jim was no fledgling to take a dare and step within reach of those bronze arms. The man's fingers looked strong enough to pull out an opponent's muscles as an ape pulls off a chicken's head, and the candlelight was in his favor.

"Shoot him, Jimgrim; shoot him!"

Suliman, with no affairs of state to complicate the issue, could imagine only that one remedy.

"Are you afraid to? Give me the pistol. I am not afraid."

The *iblis* answered that by putting out his tongue between his teeth, screwing his face into a hideous likeness of the prince of darkness, and hissing like an angry cat. Suliman screamed and jumped back against the far wall.

"Shoot, Jimgrim! If he spits and it hits you, you will die!"

The *iblis* took the hint and spat, wide of the mark on purpose, as a warship fires an "angry blank" across another's bows. Past master of bluff and opportunity; he was too wise to spit straight and prove his ammunition harmless. It obviously disconcerted him that Jim stood still.

"What do you want?" he demanded.

"Nothing more than I can have," Jim answered.

"Fool!" sneered the *iblis*. "He who wants no more than that is like the rat that craves a bellyful. Get out of here. *Ruh min hene!*"

"Not until I have what I can have."

"What is it then?"

"Partnership."

"Thou—dog of an Arab—son of a mother of abominations—spat-upon offspring of sixty dogs—fuel for the fire of Eblis—partnership with me?"

"Aye, with you, father of impotent curses."

The *iblis* laughed again.

"Shoot!" he jeered. "No bullet can harm me."

And whether the man really believed that or not Jim was at a loss to know. A deal of fanatical self-confidence goes to the attainment of such dancing and deviltry as his.

"The bark of the pistol will bright my friends in any case," said Jim.

"The bark of a jackal summons the pack to eat carrion," the *iblis* answered; "but one roar of a lion sends them scurrying."

Jim pointed the pistol straight at him, and met his eyes along the blued steel barrel. The *iblis* did not flinch, and Jim felt in rather a predicament. He, too, was bluffing, for he had not the slightest intention of killing the man—even in self-defense if he could help it.

Dead the rascal would be useless. Alive there was the possibility of making him uncover all the ramifications of his plans. If Jim managed to call Catesby and Narayan Singh they could easily capture the man between the three of them. By gagging him and waiting near the cave they might even secure a few of the thieves when they came to deliver loot.

But Jim knew better than to suppose that this imitation leper was without influential backing, and he wanted the "men higher up." One or two words that Jenkins dropped had convinced him that the brigadier was making use of the most tempting of all tools to the unscrupulous ambitious man—the criminal network of the underworld, and he did not propose to play into Jenkins' hands by destroying the evidence too soon.

He suspected that nothing would suit the brigadier's purpose better at the moment than to have this particular tool safely under lock and key. The *iblis* had served his purpose by producing a condition, out of which Jenkins proposed to get credit by destroying it and then attributing the blame to his superiors, adopting the U.S. brand of cheap city politics transported to another sphere, without quite all the subtlety or half the brains.

"Better shoot soon," grinned the *iblis*, probably mistaking Jim's deliberation for superstitious funk.

Jim lowered the pistol. He decided to summon his two friends by other means.

"Suliman," he said, "come here a minute."

But Suliman had had enough of it and had vanished, creeping like a ghost among the shadows. A moment later he heard the boy scramble out of the passage into the entrance and take to his heels.

"The child is wiser than the man," the *iblis* grinned maliciously.

Jim went to the entrance and leaned with his back against the opening, cutting off the one way of retreat and hoping that the *iblis* might not force the issue by attacking him. For he was fully resolved not to shoot if that could be avoided by any means; and strong though he knew himself to be he suspected that the *iblis* had twice his strength.

More depended on Suliman in the next few minutes than he cared to dwell on, and he went through the alternating cold chills and hot sweat that always attacked him when success or failure depended for the moment on someone else. It was Jim's besetting weakness that he could not rest easily unless the key to a given crisis were in his own hand, and he suffered more in such minutes than a victim on the rack.

There were so many possibilities. Suliman might even be killed by a leopard. A hyena might overcome natural cowardice sufficiently to attack a boy of that size. Or he might lose his way.

Catesby and Narayan Singh might have grown impatient and have tried to follow, in which case Suliman might fail to find them. Perhaps they were already scouting in the wrong direction. Or lurking thieves might make away with the boy. If the camp-thieves should return and catch him alone with the *iblis* he would be in a fine predicament.

And all the while the *iblis* sat quite still, blinking beside the candle in what, if not amusement, was a most astounding bluff at it. Insolently naked, impudently confident, he seemed aware of hidden resources of which Jim knew nothing.

He was certainly an unusual malefactor. Nine criminals out of ten caught in a corner and held at pistol-point would have at least pretended to consider that partnership proposal, if only with a view to subsequent treachery. In fact, all that redeemed the proposal itself from treachery was certainty that the *iblis* would never dream of playing fair. Jim might have gained an insight into the inner workings of the scheme while the other sought to gain time, that was all.

"When your friends come they will be as impotent as you are," said the *iblis* after a few minutes.

His tone of voice was that of an agent of the Inquisition discussing the next item on the program for a victim's benefit.

It was tempting to answer threat with threat, but that is a poor game. Threats are always launched either to unmask the other's batteries or else to undermine self-command and blind an opponent to his wisest course. There is not exception to that rule, even though threateners don't always analyze it and the threatened seldom do.

Feeling like a bear that has treed his man, Jim waited in expectant silence, little guessing, in spite of all his hard-won understanding of Eastern human nature, what a consummate player of surprise hands he had to deal with.

"Allah makes all things easy. I can deal three or four of you as easily as one," remarked the *iblis* after a long silence.

Jim did not answer.

"I can deal with twenty-five as easily as one."

"Why not deal with one first, while you have the chance?" laughed Jim.

For answer to that the *iblis* pressed out the candle with his thumb and threw the cave into instant, utter blackness. He did not make a sound, but by the time Jim could get the flashlight form his pocket and press the button there was no sigh of him anywhere. He had vanished as completely as the darkness did under the electric glare.

Jim gripped his pistol and flashed the light all over the cave, turning the rays into the other recesses one by one. As far as he could see from where he stood they all seemed empty, but he did not dare leave his place by the entrance to look more carefully because that would have given the *iblis* a chance to bolt. If there was a passage leading through one of the recesses into another cave he could afford to wait and look for that after the arrival of Catesby and Narayan Singh, because however many their ramifications, those ancient tombs of Palestine never have more than one small opening to the world outside.

He kept the light turned steadily on the floor in front of him to guard against surprise, and presently he knew why the *iblis* had chosen just that moment for disappearance. Jim's own ears are exceptionally sharp, but the other's must have been sharper.

He could hear approaching footsteps now. Catesby and Narayan Singh were coming.

He did not look around to greet them. From somewhere in the coal-black shadow of one of the recesses the *iblis* began barking like a jackal. Most fanatics use some form or other of animal noise to goad themselves into action. He kept his eyes alert in front of him and, since he did not choose to betray his nationality to the *iblis* yet, called aloud to his friends in Arabic.

"*Ta'ala, islab; ma fi darar!* (Come on, you fellows; there's nothing the matter!)"

The *iblis* barked again, and footsteps in the winding tunnel behind him doubled their speed. He set his back more squarely against the opening, for if the *iblis* proposed to make a rush for if the *iblis* proposed to make a rush for liberty now was his last chance; or his active muscle might count on surprise and speed to upset men groping through a narrow passage with the light behind them.

The *iblis* changed his bark into a yell. Jim stiffened himself for action. Less than a second later a hand reached forward from behind him and seized his throat in a grip there was no breaking. He tried to fire backward over his shoulder, but another hand seized his wrist and nearly broke it, wrenching the pistol free.

Then two men jumped on him, and when the steely fingers on his throat had squeezed him half-unconscious they bound both wrists behind him with a leather thong and threw him face downward on the floor. There he lay still, making no effort yet to look about him, concentrating all his faculties on regaining breath and recovering from the physical pain. He was stunned, hurt and ashamed of himself for being taken by surprise; and as soon as he could breathe without agony he battled down and beat the unmanning suggestions of self-accusation that have put many more stout men out of business than ever surprise or defeat did.

"Shall we cut his throat?" inquired a gruff-voice casually.

There was no immediate answer. Jim lay with the gooseflesh rising and receding on his back in tidal waves, while an Arab whom he could not see stood across him with a foot on either side, ready at a nod to do the butcher work.

Someone lighted the candle-end. Another someone blew it out. There began to be whispering over in a corner. Other men came in through the tunnel and threw heavy objects on the floor, one or two of which rattled with the sound of rifle swivels.

It seemed that there was quite an argument going on, although Jim could not distinguish the voice of the *iblis*. They hissed over in the corner like a lot of snakes, once and again a low growl breaking out by way of emphasis. The man who stood athwart Jim's ribs grew restless and struck a long knife on the palm of his hand.

"Oh, let's cut his throat and be done with it," he grumbled, stooping to fumble for Jim's forehead and bend his head back for the sacrifice.

To have started to struggle at that moment would have meant death certain; the Arab would have taken the decision on himself. But it was nervous work to lie still with throat bent convex, taut and ready.

One other thought monopolized Jim's brain at that minute. Knife or no knife, he was ready to let out a yell of warning if he could catch sound of his friends' footsteps in time. If he died for it the next second, he must save them from advancing into the trap, and he listened desperately.

He thought it was all up when the whole gang began to cross the floor toward him. Then he put up the best fight possible, which wasn't much in the circumstances. Just before the first man reached him he rose to his knees with a jerk and tossed the would-be executioner over his head.

The man who had annexed his flashlight discovered how to turn it on, but held it sidewise, and nine men stood revealed, all eyes turned on the new toy. Jim charged the nearest of them head forward and butted him in the belly, sending him sprawling. But the rest fell on him, tripped him up, beat him and pulled a bag over his head.

They bound a cloth tightly over his mouth outside the bag, and a moment later he was being hustled out of the cave, pricked on from behind by the knife-point of the wrathful one who had been butted.

"By Allah!" growled an angry voice behind him. "There shall be a high price exacted for that ram's pleasantry! By morning you shall wish *Um Kulsum* (an utterly unrighteous harridan of Arab legend) had never brought you forth."

CHAPTER VIII

"Allah makes all things easy!"

Jim had not the least idea where they were taking him. His trained sense of direction was checkmated by a simple precaution that they took outside the cave, pushing him from one to the other and spinning him in a sort of savage blindman's buff. To end that ignominy he lay down at last, whereat they kicked and dragged him up again and hurried on their way.

It was all he could do to breathe through the combination of gag and gunny-bag. That effort and the pain in his wrist kept his normally keen intuition in abeyance; but he did experience the sensation of passing between high walls, and suspected accordingly that their course lay south, along the *wady* through which he had reached the tomb. He could not tell whether the *iblis* was with them or not. The very few words that passed were in a low whisper. But by the jingle of metal on metal he knew that some of his captors were carrying looted rifles; and once they stopped to gather up something heavy and several of them carried along afterward in turns between them. Whatever that load might be, they drove away jackals from it before stopping to pick it up.

Supposing that his surmise was correct that they were hurrying down the *wady*, then he was sure that they turned nearly due west at the end of it; but after that the windings of the course were altogether too mazy to remember. He had begun by counting his steps from the point where they left off hazing him, but realized the uselessness of that after the eighth or ninth turn.

Strangely enough, in spite of the gag and the pain in his wrist he was fairly cheerful. If they had proposed to kill him, he argued, they would have done it in the tomb; and it was his natural New England-born conviction that no set of circumstances are irretrievable until so proven. He even saw humor in the situation, now that he was sure that Catesby and Narayan Singh would not rush headlong into ambush.

He could not smile or even chuckle under the smothering gag; but mirth does not really need expression, as the red man knew, who regarded laughter as womanly weakness. The imaginary picture of Suliman's rage on finding the cave empty—of Catesby's better bread chagrin—and of Narayan Singh's grim, muttered vengefulness gave him the full feeling of laughter without its compromising form.

Even in that predicament he did not think with any approval of the prospect of swift death for the *iblis*. He wanted facts first; after those let come what might.

Jim has altogether peculiar qualities that some consider cold-blooded; it never gave him the slightest twinge of satisfaction to see a criminal land in jail at the end of a long battle between wits, nor yet to see a murderer hung. What interested him at the moment—and so deeply that he would rather die than fail to unearth the lowest root of it—was the scheme behind the criminal. He had a sort of sporting admiration for the man himself, provided only he was game, much as a real hunter has a friendly feeling for the animal that does its fighting utmost.

Nevertheless it amused him to imagine the *iblis* fool enough to wait there in the tomb and be discovered by Narayan Singh. Narayan Singh knew no such nice distinctions; his was the direct, unwavering desire to get his man, with death as the only logical and satisfying finish to a criminal career.

The *iblis* would likely learn quite a lot about physical pain if he should fall into the Sikh's hands and refuse to give information; with his own wrist aching like a tooth that thought did not exactly make Jim worry.

Unless you kill outright a man who can amuse himself in that way, thinking of other things in spite of his predicament while captors hurry him helpless toward an unimaginable fate, you never can have the best of him. For he is not mesmerized by circumstance. Fear gets no chance to do its paralyzing work. Though the fact seems exactly the reverse, the odds are really in his favor.

Jim's captors were obsessed by the knowledge that they had a prisoner who must be disposed of in some way; and the longer they put him off the less simple and convenient the solution was going to seem. Jim, on the other hand, was thinking of anything except that prospect, so that when the next development was staged he faced it quite unconvinced of desperation.

Most captors imagine they had imprisoned a man's wits when they have tied his hands, and many prisoners believe it too; but the wise man when he is bound thinks of "Shakespeare and the musical glasses" until his moment comes. Jim began to consider the probably past history of that cavernous tomb he had left, while they hustled him through the darkness and worried one another with horse whisperings.

* * * *

They crossed the railway at last, for he tripped twice on the metals, which meant that they had turned from the west or thereabouts to very nearly due east. Ten minutes' hurry after that brought them to some sort of stone building, where they let him lean against the wall while one of the party wrestled with a rusty lock and key.

He tried to work his hands loose by rubbing the thong against the stonework, but made small progress because of the pain in his wrist, and only succeeded in working off his scarab ring.

The door swung open at last on creaking hinges. Two men took him by the shoulders and thrust him forward. He tripped on a stone still, and they jeered as he landed face downward on a rough stone floor. A second later the door slammed shut behind him and he heard the scream of the complaining key.

He lay still and listened for several minutes to discover whether he was alone or not. Hearing nothing, he scrambled to his feet and, backing until he reached the wall, began to feel his way along it, hunting some projection against which he might chafe the leather thong. The room he was in was circular, which set him thinking.

Part way around the circuit he felt some steps, and a rusty iron rod supporting the handrail. There were better tools that that for cutting rawhide, but the rawhide was eating into his wrists, and necessity sharpens patience.

First against the edge of a stone step, then against the rusty iron, then against the step again, he chafed and sawed, injuring his own skin almost as often as the leather, and without any means of measuring progress. During a pause while he strained at the thong to test it he heard a sound that seemed familiar.

In a flash his thought went back to the entrance of the tomb and the dry, peculiar noise that had induced him to enter. It sounded like the same cough or belch or whatever it was. Yet he could hear no breathing.

He changed the order of proceedings then and knelt, working his face up and down against the step to get the gag off, and succeeded after several minutes in forcing it down over his chin, where it hung loose. But it was not so simple to get the bag off his head. He managed that finally by bending his head downward and shaking it until the blood surged up behind his eyes and the universe seemed like a sea of fire with purple stars in it.

It was a minute after he had got rid of the sack before he could see at all, although the circular room in which he found himself was not absolutely dark. Faint moonlight filtered through a small iron-barred window set twelve feet above the floor, and dimly illuminated the bare walls.

He stared about him for another minute before his eyes recovered sufficiently to make out a shadowy shape beneath the window. Little by little, as he grew accustomed to the dim light, he made out the outline of a man, who sat so still as to seem dead, although it was an uncommon posture for a dead man, squatting Moslem-fashion, elbow on knee. He was about to approach to investigate when the man moved, and then he recognized the *iblis*.

The movement was in character. He had been sitting shrouded in a brown cloak, but threw it back now from his shoulders and sat naked, eyeing Jim with scornful curiosity, much as he might have watched the antics of a beetle on a pin. Jim set his back against the steps and resumed his labor at the thong, pressing hard and rubbing with as little noise as possible.

"I can deal with you with your hands free," said the *iblis* after a minute or two.

"Try it," Jim suggested, and threw caution to the winds.

Pretending to chafe more violently at the thong, measure the distance with his eyes meanwhile, he went for the *iblis* with a sudden run and jump, intending to land feet foremost on him. But without any obvious muscular effort, the *iblis* shifted his position just as suddenly half a yard to the right, and Jim's feet hit the wall.

He made a prodigious effort to recover balance and jump again, but fell on his back, and having lost his Arab headdress when he shook the bag free, contact with the stone floor nearly stunned him. So he lay still, and the *iblis* leaned down to peer into his face, with that unchanging, curiously scornful smile that was half-sneer, half-amusement.

"I can deal with three—or thirty—or three hundred of you."

Jim did not answer. With his hands free, half-stunned or not, he would have taken his chance in a free-for-all fight, though the *iblis* was as strong as two of him; but to tempt providence in his present position would have been sheer lunacy. He was constitutionally unable to believe himself down and out as long as consciousness remained, so he lay and wondered whence his opportunity would come and what form it would take.

The *iblis* provided it. He was evidently of an economical turn of mind, for he produced from a pocket in the discarded cloak the self-same stub of candle that had served his purpose in the tomb, and lit it. Jim set his teeth, thinking at first that torture was to be the next item on the program; for in the fingers of an expert a lighted candle can do as much mischief as a red-hot iron. But the *iblis* only looked about for a place to set the light on, and leaned over finally to drip wax on the floor and stick it there out of reach.

So Jim scrambled to his feet again. The *iblis* looked up at him and laughed.

"See what is upstairs," he suggested.

"Untie my wrists!" said Jim.

The *iblis* did it, not troubling to get to his feet but turning Jim around and unknotting the thong with fingers that were strong enough to have unraveled wire. Standing, chafing his wrists to restore circulation and get some of the pain out of the swollen one, Jim realized how utterly helpless he would be if he tried to fight. It was true that he had boots on and could kick, but unless you are very certain of your aim, and equally sure of surprising your adversary, one blow wins no battle.

So he decided to try the stairs and see. But the *iblis* sprang across the room in front of him and prevented him by sitting on the bottom step.

"Not now," he grinned.

"Why the change of mind?"

"Go back to the wall and sit down."

Jim went back and leaned against the wall, holding his hot wrist against the cool stone, grateful for any way of gaining time, for time was obviously in his favor. For one thing, Catesby would probably report him missing; and Narayan Singh would certainly not rest until he had found him dead or alive.

If he could only guess what the *iblis'* purpose was in bringing him to that place he would have a great deal more than time in his favor, for the man with definite plans and a nefarious purpose is always at a disadvantage as compared to an equally determined man aware of both plan and purpose and bent on spoiling both.

He felt his way along the wall to the door and tested the lock while he weighed the situation in his mind. The lock was set into an immensely heavy wooden door and was unbreakable without tools; but a little enlightenment dawned as he watched the *iblis*, who sat smiling at his futile effort to escape.

Upstairs there was probably loot—most likely rifles. That would account for the *iblis* being willing for him to go up there with his hands tied, and unwilling otherwise. Supposing that only five per cent of the loot stolen from the British camp in the last month or two was up there, the *iblis* certainly would not carry it away alone, and probably would not dare leave it where it was much longer. Therefore it was likely that he was waiting for men, who would come before morning to remove the stuff; nobody would be fool enough to run that risk after daybreak.

Jim's spirits began to rise. If his guess was correct, then he was on the trail of something vastly more important than the mere thieves. The ultimate receivers of the loot were worth all risks to bring to book. Certainly the *iblis* could be nothing more than a mere agent, because a naked dervish trying to dispose of rifles for any purpose or in any market would fall foul of the law within an hour, even if he tried to employ agents on his own account. There was somebody higher up—not a doubt of it.

It began to seem wisest to play the other fellow's game and wait patiently, if only because that might force the *iblis* to move next and show something of his hand. He might be a lunatic like many another pseudo-religious sensation-maker; but it was much more likely that he was a very shrewd expert in human nature, busily applying all the simple principles he knew, after the fashion of a drill-sergeant, or a jailer, or a trainer of wild beasts. His strength was circumstantial and physical; all the conditions were in his favor, as much as if he had deliberately decoyed his prisoner to chosen ground. His weak points were two—vanity and time.

So Jim sat down. And curiosity took hold of him so completely as to obliterate the pain in his wrists along with all sense of his own danger. Satisfied that the *iblis* had a definite objective and a motive behind every move, he cared for nothing but to discover what they were.

The same spirit that had made him study Arabic until he knew the language better than most Arabs did, gripped him in the same way that the laboratory scientist is seized. It would have annoyed him at that moment to be discovered by his friends and rescued.

"Don't forget; his two weak points are time and vanity!"

That thought was like a formula running through the mind of a chemist bending over his retorts.

Even vanity was not strong enough to blind the *iblis* to the element of time, although it made him so sure of his own perceptive faculty that he never suspected his prisoner might be other than a local Arab. It was evidently no part of his plan to waste time letting the sense of mystery grow thin.

"Allah makes all things easy," he announced again. "I can tell your father's name and your mother's, and the name of the village you come from."

If Jim's curiosity had been of a non-scientific turn he would have dared the man to do it; and the *iblis* no doubt would have side-stepped by refusing to commit himself. He would not have been one step nearer to discovery.

"Vanity and time—vanity and time—those are his weak points!"

Time could look after itself, for the minutes go by changeless measure. Jim decided to tickle vanity, which is usually dangerous until well fed.

"That is indeed a great gift," he said respectfully. "I remember that you called me by my right name in the tomb tonight. To be able to tell a man's name, and those of his father and mother, and his village—that is wonderful!"

"Allah makes all things easy," smiled the *iblis* self-complacently. "I not only have gifts, I confer them. I not only have power, I can pass it on to others."

There was something vaguely familiar about that statement. Jim had heard it, not exactly in those words, but near enough, in a back room in Boston where an occultist held forth; and again in New York City in a barroom where a political gang-leader held brief sway. Only this man, being half-savage and believing he dealt with another like himself, made his boasts a little bit more definite. Possibly, like the politician and the occultist, he half believed his own assertions.

"How does a man attain such gifts?" Jim asked him.

"It is all in the Koran," said the *iblis*. "Allah makes all things easy."

"They say that all knowledge is written in the Koran," Jim answered. "But who shall understand it?"

"Ah!"

The *iblis* chuckled from the depths of his immense conceit.

"There is no profit in ignorance. But there is wisdom in obeying those who understand."

"And you understand? Shall I obey you?"

"You *must* obey me. I could kill you here—now—with these fingers."

That was probably perfectly true. Jim did not choose to dispute it; he would have had as much chance against a gorilla.

"I could let you go and cause you to drop dead within fifty paces," continued the *iblis*. "I, who know your name, and your birthplace, can curse them all and—"

"No, no!" Jim protested. It was just as easy to pretend terror as to laugh. "Don't do that! In the name of Allah, Lord of Creatures, don't do that!"

"Then obey me."

"I must. What else can I do? You have made me afraid," said Jim, wondering just how many superstitious potential thieves had been initiated in that room.

"If you disobey in one thing you shall turn to worms—in one day—in two days—in three days—according to the measure of disobedience."

That was clever. Every victim was sure to disobey in some particular, but delay in fulfillment of the overhanging threat could only be held to qualify the disobedience, and the fear would remain.

"For disobedience you shall turn to worms. Your roof shall fall in. Your relatives shall die of want."

"But what if I obey?" Jim asked him.

"Ah!"

The *iblis* chuckled again, as if reviewing in his mind the wondrous list of prizes.

"Those who are obedient have protection. Provided with protection they may help themselves. Allah makes all things easy!"

"Why do you pretend to be a leper?" Jim asked suddenly and at that the *iblis* flew into such a rage that every muscle in his huge frame trembled.

His eyes blazed. His lips, thrust outward like an ape's, uncovered yellow teeth that could have crushed a forearm. Fingers strong enough to pluck out a victim's sinews one by one twitched with desire, and his long toes kept time with them. Suddenly he spat, writhing up his face into hideous contortions, and hissing as he had done in the cave.

"Cursed dog of an unbelieving fool!" he snarled. "Son of sixty dogs and a cesspool! Impudent, insolent, abominable lump of earth about to perish! Bloodless, loveless, senseless, hopeless *pig!* Eater of worms and dung! Idiot!"

Foam bubbled through his teeth and ran down on his chin in slime. It was not difficult to be afraid of him.

"Come and touch me! Come and see how soon I can make you a leper!"

Not to obey, of course, was disobedience. On the other hand, to obey would be to call the bluff, which might oblige the *iblis* to take some unimaginably desperate course. There was no guessing what tricks he had in store, so Jim played safe.

"No, no!" he begged. "In the name of Allah the compassionate, not that!"

"I can make *abras* (leprous) whom I will!"

That was Jim's cue to do a little sensational acting. Plainly the purpose was to make him thoroughly afraid, so to get at the motive behind the purpose he would have to seem afraid; and he set to work to do that. Most of Jim's successes had been won by keeping his head in emergencies; he had not much experience of the outward effects of terror on himself. He had to risk overacting the part, putting in practice all he could remember of the symptoms of Arab panic.

His teeth stubbornly refused to chatter, and he could not make the cold sweat come; but he could slobber and mutter Koran text and beg for mercy, throwing himself forward to beat on the floor with the palms of his hands and call the *iblis* such names as "prince of wizards—lord of potent curses—father of terrors and captain of calamities," names which pleased the *iblis* very much indeed.

After that he flew into a panic, making believe he thought the *iblis* would rush at him. He scrambled to his feet and hugged the wall like an animal trying to escape, then beat on the door with his fists, and finally came to a stand with open mouth and glaring eyes as if hope were gone and he could only await the inevitable.

The *iblis* appeared to consider himself a judge of such symptoms, and was not quite satisfied yet. He, too, seemed to await the inevitable, as if fear always ran an appointed course and he preferred to see the thing complete.

Jim, aping abject terror, stood and wondered what the hell the man expected more. What should an Arab in fear of witchcraft do in proof of utter lack of self-control? He had it! He sprang at the candle and stamped out the light with his foot, screaming instantly in added terror of darkness and scrambling around the wall to the door again to bear on it and shout for help.

At last the *iblis* appeared satisfied. It was time to turn the last trick.

"Allah makes all things easy. I can find you in the dark!" he boomed.

In answer Jim groaned and muttered enough to satisfy the very hellions who stoke the fires of Eblis.

"I can make you *abras* without touching you!"

"Oh no, no, no! *Shi mamkut! Mnain hashshakawi!* (That is abominable! How could you be so wicked!)"

"Or I can spare you if I will."

"Spare me then, father of afflictions!"

"Or I can spare you for a little while, and reach you with my curses at a distance if you disobey me."

"Damn him, I wish he'd hurry up," thought Jim. "I'm getting tired of this."

But he managed to keep up a pretty good semblance of terror; and either the *iblis* was getting tired, too, or else time began to press.

"Be still. I will spare for the present."

"*Ilham'dillah!*' (God be praised!)

Jim collapsed into a squatting posture on the floor, moving his head this and that way to try and see the other in the dark; but the *iblis'* black skin made that impossible. Apparently, however, the *iblis* could see Jim and guessed his purpose.

"I can be invisible whenever I choose."

"O father of darkness, what do you want with me?"

"Ah! What do I want with you? What but to make of you a wizard like myself. I recognize the spirit of obedience, but there must be a test."

"Father of terrors, I have been too much tested!"

"*Malaish.* (No matter.) There is another. Fail in this and you shall see the leprosy seize you in an hour."

Having exhausted all the outward forms of fear he could think of, Jim sat still.

"My servants will come presently," said the *iblis*. "They are not such as you, fit to become wizards, but servants—mean men—dogs. They will take things away from here to another place. Go with them, but say nothing to them. Answer no questions. Watch where they put the things. Then return and bring word of it to me."

"I obey, father of happenings," Jim answered meekly.

It was almost the hardest thing he ever did to keep a note of triumph from his voice that minute.

"Speak one word to them—answer on question—and the curse shall rot the carcasses of you and yours!"

"I am silent—silent!"

"Then *be* silent!"

For another half hour Jim and the *iblis* faced each other in darkness, Jim on the floor with his back against the wall and the *iblis* on the bottom step. What with headache, hunger, pain in his wrist and general weariness Jim almost fell asleep; but just as the first false light before dawn brightened the narrow window there came a stealthy, subdued knocking on the door that brought the *iblis* to his feet. He crossed the room, put on his brown cloak, produced an enormous key, went to listen at the door, and after a backward, precautionary glance in Jim's direction opened it.

CHAPTER IX

"The butcha *speaks wisdom."*

Catesby and Narayan Singh had no more matches; and Suliman had none, for they searched him. They tried to fathom the cave's recesses in the dark, but gave that up as hopeless; even the Sikh's eyes could not penetrate the Stygian darkness that began where the faintly reflected starlight ceased, a yard or two from the entrance hole.

So they climbed out, and with Suliman disconsolate on Narayan Singh's knees held a consultation. Catesby, of course, began it.

"Which shall we do? Return to camp and report Major Grim missing, or hunt about and try to find him?"

But Suliman spoke next, being only a stickler for etiquette when he could score by it.

"I will not go back to camp! If that *iblis* has eaten Jimgrim, then Narayan Singh must kill the *iblis* and cut his belly open and let Jimgrim out."

Catesby laughed, but Narayan Singh knew better. It is not only the children in that land who believe in goblin stories.

"If we go back to camp without him, *sahib*, half the camp will call us liars and the other half will believe henceforth all the tales about the *iblis*, and twice as many more tales of their own invention. Moreover, my orders are to bring that Jimgrim back to Jerusalem alive."

"But where to look?" wondered Catesby.

There was cactus-covered sandy hill and dale in every direction. They might chance on footprints, but likely enough it would be easier and quicker work to follow rumor through Jerusalem city than such a trail by moonlight.

"Let us ask the *butcha*," said Narayan Singh, preferring to be charged with talking nonsense rather than seem to rebuke an officer.

Etiquette in his case was something only to be broken in a pinch.

Catesby produced a cigarette, and swore, remembering he had no matches. Narayan Singh, with mutiny in mind if Catesby should insist on going back to camp, proceeded after a fashion of his own to draft a proposition.

"Now Suliman-jee, son of the warrior Rustum, how much have you learned from Jimgrim?"

"Everything."

"That is a very great deal. Tell me some of it. Where would thieves sell loot, for instance?"

"In the *suk* (bazaar)."

"That might be. But if they feared to go into the *suk*, what then?"

"They might run away over the hills to Hebron."

"In that case we cannot follow them tonight. But if they were going to the *suk*, would they go by night?"

"No."

"Why not, father of ready answers?"

"They would be shot. None but thieves enter a town by night."

"And if they had loot with them, would they wait to be caught with it?"

"They would bury it, or hide it somewhere."

"And then—what then?"

"One or two would go into the town at daybreak. Later a cart would come, or a camel, or an ox; and the loot would be taken to the *suk* by daylight, covered up. That is how all the thieves behave."

"Father of good scouting! And would they hide the loot on this side of the railway track, or beyond?"

"That is a foolish question. If they hid it on this side, whoever came afterward to fetch it would have to carry it across the track by daylight, and the track is always watched."

"True, father of knavery! Whereas between the track and the town—?"

"Who would search a cart or a camel between the town and the railway line? The car leaves town and returns; that is nothing. It is carts and camels crossing the track that are always searched."

"True. True. At night thieves could cross the track unseen—"

"Easily."

"But they could not enter the town unseen. That is so. And if we should watch the open land between the railway and the town at daybreak, we might learn something. Do you hear him, *sahib*? The butcha *speaks* wisdom."

Catesby yawned, and then laughed.

"All right, Narayan Singh. I see your mind's set on not going back to camp. Suits me. Better a night in the open than a lame tale for General Jenkins! Besides, I like your kind of guts. Come on, we'll head for the railway line."

* * * *

The Sikh carried Suliman, who promptly fell asleep with his head hanging downward over the stalwart shoulder like a dead sheep's, swinging in time to the stride.

"That kid's a nuisance," Catesby commented. "However, I suppose he can't be expected to wake up and walk in this sand, and we can't leave him. I'll carry him turn about with you."

"Nay, *sahib*, it is nothing. Let him sleep. In the morning when he wakes he may serve a purpose."

But full rations ever since Jim had rescued him from starving in the Jaffa Gate had filled out the boy's stocky frame, and it was no easy matter to carry him for mile after mile across that loose desert land. Even when they came to cultivation the going was still heavy, and Catesby took his turn, wondering after five minutes of it at the Sikh's endurance.

They had to put the boy down, and wake him, and make him walk when they neared the railway because, being in Arab costume, they were certain to be fired at unless they took cover and watched their chance. Finally, after slinking for half an hour among long shadows, they crawled through a culvert and emerged on the far side without being challenged, although two Gurkas on patrol passed within ten yards of where they hid.

Within three hundred paces of them, then, was a cluster of ruined buildings, shot to pieces in the war and never since rebuilt, but patched here and there as if someone had tried to make them habitable. In the moonlight, they looked like a medieval castle with its upper story gone, for part of what might have been the keep reared jagged and broken above the rest.

"What is that place, *sahib*?" asked Narayan Singh.

"Nothing much. It used to be an Arab village with a mosque in the middle. Our guns shelled it, and most of it was burned. That tower you see is all that's left of the minaret. Nobody uses the place now."

"Hah!"

The Sikh's one monosyllable suggested a world of reservations rather than assent.

"That place'll be full of lice and bedbugs," Catesby warned.

"Aye, and these days the peace have made us fat, *sahib*. They will have good feasting! The top of that broken tower is the place from which to watch."

"Come on, then. Let's get bitten."

But it was not easy to reach the buildings without risking being seen by sentries on patrol, and they had to crawl under cover of a ridge of sandy earth that held more thorns and insects to the square yard than a brush has bristles. Then a pariah dog smelled them and yelped to the pack, and for five minutes they were the center of abominable noise.

They did not dare shoot, any more than the curs dared come close enough to be killed with a stick. Throwing lumps of dirt and sticks only increased the yelping; and there weren't any stones. But finally another pariah yelped in the distance and the pack raced off to fight him for his find.

After that it was an easy matter to approach the ruined mosque, but quite another task to climb the tower. The cluttered village street was all in shadow, but the moon shone full on the mosque wall, showing it all in ruins with the broken tower beside it, erect and unclimbable.

The place was of typical Arab "culture"—jumbled, tumbled, cluttered, evil-smelling, verminous; war had only multiplied the normal chaos. That minaret had been the only decent building, and it remained the only thing worth anybody's trouble.

There was one little slit of a window visible almost directly facing the moon. It looked faintly luminous.

"D'you suppose there's glass in it?" asked Catesby. "Does that look like reflected light to you?"

Narayan Singh scouted closed to investigate. The window was much too high to reach, but he climbed on a broken wall to reach its level and returned at the end of ten minutes, stopping on his way to examine the ground close to the door. A slash of while across the blackness of his beard betrayed that he was pleased with the result.

"I heard no sound, *sahib*; but there is no glass, and there is a light within. Moreover, I found this."

He put a scarab ring into Catesby's hand.

"Jimgrim *sahib's!*" cried the Sikh.

"How d'you know? They're common enough. It might be anyone's."

"Ask the *butcha*."

Suliman examined it and grew exited at once.

"*Taib!* That is Jimgrim's. I have cleaned it for him fifty times."

"I suppose they've killed him."

Catesby had been too much of late under the brigadier's harrow to be an optimist.

"Nay, *sahib*. More likely he dropped it there for me to find. If they had killed him we should have found his naked body in the cave or thereabouts. If they had looted the ring and dropped it when they reached this place, they would have missed it and have looked. It lay in full moonlight on the flat side of a broken stone against the wall."

"Then I go," said Suliman, "to break that door down with this *kukri*."

"*Ahsti, ahsti!*" said the Sikh. "What is your judgment, *sahib*?"

* * * *

Catesby was in high spirits again.

It took a Jenkins to depress him, and not much more than a symptom of encouragement to set him up.

"No sense in rushing things. If he's dead, he's dead. If he's alive in there we'll get him. Is there another door?"

"None, *sahib*. I saw all around the place."

"Then we'll watch this one until morning, and creep up close enough to hear if anything happens. Look about for a beam to have handy in case we should want to burst the door in."

Together they pulled a roof-beam out from a mess of fallen thatch, and laid it where they could find it in the dark that would shut down when the moonlight waned. Then Narayan Singh crept close to the door and listened. He was grinning again when he returned.

"He is in there, and alive. I heard his voice. I could not hear the words. He seemed to be close to the door and to be carrying on a conversation. Shall I go back and rap on the door softly as a signal?"

"No. It might be the signal for his death. How many voices did you hear?"

"One other."

"He'd be sure to yell if they tried to murder him. In that case, down with the door. But if we go to his rescue before he needs us we might spoil his game."

"*Atcha, sahib*," said the Sikh; but he examined both pistols again and plainly did not like the inactivity.

It relieved his anxiety a little, however, when Catesby chose a black hole to hide in among the tumbled ruins of the mosque within twenty paces of the minaret door.

* * * *

Nobody who has not tried it, out hunting or in war, can guess how hard it is to listen attentively and scratch himself at the same time. Suliman, who not so many months ago had been clothed in little else than paupers' lice and had hardly had time to forget the indifference that goes with it, suffered least. Perhaps, too, his carcass was less appetizing.

But the Sikh is a clean race, prone to look down on even the tubbed and scrubbed British officer as none too particular. And that heap of ruins was alive with myriads of body-insects, "whose seed is in themselves" and that exist apparently eternally on nothing until warm-blooded provender arrives.

Yet they did not dare move away. The moon was too low in the sky, and whoever had brought Jim to that place would likely to make a move of some kind before morning, or at least soon after sunrise. If this were a rendezvous of thieves, whoever approached it would likely do some careful scouting in advance. There was nothing for it by to lie still and scratch—and swear—and scratch.

The Sikh's ears were sharpest, and once he swore he heard the voice of a man begging for mercy.

"Maybe Jimgrim has a man down?" ventured Suliman.

But the other two grew nervous, and this time it was Catesby who crawled to the door to listen while Narayan Singh watched the coast. Catesby, too, distinguished the voices of two men, or thought he did; but the door was too thick for him to hear one word or establish Jim's identity. He crept back again into hiding in that divided frame of mind from which small comfort ever comes, wondering what he would think of himself should it turn out afterward that Jim had been all along in peril of his life—already dead perhaps; yet recalling Jim's words earlier that night, that it would be better to wait for a week than spoil things by a false move.

When dawn came, what with insects and indecision they were thoroughly miserable, stiff, sore, hungry and depressed by the zero-hour self-consciousness that sheds the drear light of cold unreason on every circumstance. Suliman, who had been blubbering, fell asleep again.

Catesby's thoughts were back on Jenkins and the hopelessness of clearing himself of a false charge in view of the brigadier's notorious ability to lie plausibly. Narayan Singh was squatting with eyes half-closed, dreaming in another language and another dimension, for that matter; not even the Sikhs can tell each other what thoughts reach them when the far-away look settles on their faces.

None of them saw the morning visitors arrive until the twelfth and last of them came abreast and the first one struck the door with cautious knuckles. They were ordinary-looking *fellaheen*—villagers, that is—and each man carried some ordinary-looking load or other—baskets, mats, bags, a patchwork quilt.

The last man led a donkey—one of those bruised and tortured little insects that make less noise than a ghost and eat endless Arab blows and insult in return for overwork. None of the men had a weapon as far as it was possible to see; for lack of the customary thick club the last man used his fist on the donkey's nose as a hint that it was time to stand still.

The leading man knocked half a dozen times; then the door opened and they all filed in, but from where the watchers lay it was not possible to see who opened it. The donkey went in too, and the lock squealed again behind her.

There followed further agonies of indecision and impatience; for, weapons or no weapons, there is no limit at all to the senseless cruelty of which the *fellaheen* are capable. Like their prototypes of Egypt the Palestinians have such a heritage of oppression to look back on that their actions are simply a matter of mood.

They smolder, as it were, in childlike harmlessness for periods whose probably duration no psychologist can guess; and burst out into senseless, superstitious fury without any apparent cause. Fear they understand always; fair treatment never, having no education in it. Jim would be about as safe in their hands as among sheep or wolves, whichever mood was uppermost.

It was probably intuition that held Catesby's hand. Narayan Singh was all for action—for storming the door and holding up the crowd within at pistol-point, his one obsession being that order given him half-jokingly by Colonel Goodenough to bring Jim back to Jerusalem alive. He snarled between his teeth at Catesby, urging force, and laughing. It is a bad sign when a Sikh does that.

"Hold your tongue," Catesby ordered him.

Having to control the other did him good. He realized almost for the first time how the court martial hanging over his head had lowered his own opinion of himself to a degree that the Sikh's more subtly receptive mind had found contagious. He braced himself deliberately.

Hitherto he had almost unconsciously admitted to the rule that, being technically under arrest, he was technically void of the right to command. Now he fell back on the racial issue. Right or wrong, the white man has his place above the black, and above all the grades of color whether ebony or yellow, Aryan, Mongol or Ethiopian.

Narayan Singh recognized the change. The world being what it is, a product of history, improving only gradually, men still like leaders; and the braver and more self-disciplined the man the less he appreciates a leader in whose face he may sneer with impunity.

There was absolutely nothing menial about Narayan Singh; he was a high-chinned man, who would polish his officer's boots for pride in the well-groomed officer. But the officer good enough to have his harness cleaned by him and lead him must know his own mind. He would rather be told to hold his tongue by a mistaken strong man than be allowed his own way by a weakling. If it were not so, there would be no leaders and no led.

Having made up his mind to await the event and shoulder the full responsibility, Catesby scratched himself philosophically. He was no longer a victim, nor could the fact that he was lousy lower his self-respect. Whatever he had done rightly hitherto that night was due to intuition and old habits of thinking that survive under imposed disgrace, making it impossible for a true man to become untrue, or a leader incapable of leading, except gradually, step by step.

Now it was as if a cloud of depression vanished. He did thenceforward what he consciously chose to do, captain of his own soul and master of his destiny. Even Suliman, waking drowsily, sensed the difference.

They did not wait very long. The door opened again and the donkey came forth first, loaded so heavily that it could barely stagger and showing its teeth because of the biting tightness of the cords that kept the load in place.

Over it all like a Joseph's coat of many colors they had tied the patchwork quilt, knotting it under the animal's belly; the suggestion that conveyed, whether it was intentional or not—you can't ever gage the *fellaheen's* simplicity or artfulness—was that they were honest villagers removing their household goods. Only a very suspicious observer would have balked at their having no women with them to carry the heaviest burdens.

The men filed out one by one after the donkey, each with a heavier load that he took in with him, but using what he had brought to cover or contain what he had come for—sacks—baskets—mats and an old tarpaulin knotted by the corners and carried between two men. The only remarkable difference was that whereas twelve men had entered, thirteen now came out, and there remained at least one inside to lock the door after them.

The thirteenth man looked cleaner than the rest, and carried no bundle. Also his right wrist was raw and seemed painful; and when he rubbed it with the other hand a bright red weal became visible on the left wrist too.

Suddenly Suliman leaped to his feet. Catesby clapped a hand on his mouth and dragged him down again only in the nick of time.

"Keep quiet, you little bastard!" he whispered. "Yes, I know it's Jimgrim."

He knew exactly what to do now; needed no advice or urging from Narayan Singh. He waiting only until he could speak without risk of the twelve men hearing him. There was not the slightest need to hurry. He let them go a hundred yards and disappear beyond the ruined village wall before he gave an order. Then:

"Narayan Singh, you wait here and watch the door. If anyone comes out, arrest him. If anyone else goes in, all right; wait and watch. But in that case don't let anyone out on any terms; drive 'em back with your pistol; shoot if you must, but hold 'em in there somehow until help comes. If nothing happens don't show yourself. Do you understand?"

"*Malum, sahib.*"

"Now Suliman—how long is it since you begged? Have you forgotten? Off with your boots—socks too—leave 'em here. You're dirty enough, Lord knows. Better leave your head-gear too. Tear your pants a bit; you're too well cared for to look plausible. Now some more dust in your hair. You'll do.

"Follow now, and beg from Jimgrim. Don't look back at me, and don't take no for an answer. If they turn and beat you, stick to them. Pretend you're so hungry that you don't mind being hurt. Cut along."

He lifted the youngster out of the dark hole and pitched him on to his feet outside. A moment later he followed as far as the gap in the wall. From that point he could watch what happened without any risk of being seen.

* * * *

The missionaries and police know best what perfectly con- summate actors Arab children are. Their elders have grown set in the accepted ways, so that a grown man or woman seldom varies from a given method; usually the people of one village thieve and lie to a pattern, and are all at sea when anyone gets acquainted with their habit.

But the children are less conservative, until the years bring on that eastern intellectual inertia that is partly due to Koran teach- ing and partly to polygamy. Suliman had lost none of his natural alertness yet, and he had not been long enough in Jim's control to lose delight in mischief for the sake of lawlessness.

So he accepted that part perfectly. Running until he was breathless—fingering the sweat into the corners of his eyes until it looked like tears—plucking grass as he ran, to chew and make the corners of his mouth filthy with green slime, he overtook the procession and begged alms in the name of Allah.

Nor did he go to Jim first, but singled out the owner of the donkey; for the beggar's principle is to flatter with first attention whoever had most in view of this world's goods, thus sometimes stirring a ridiculous unconscious sense of rivalry. Human nature is absurd stuff, or the beggars would all be at work producing.

Clearly those twelve men were in no mood to be generous. They cursed the boy as he approached them one by one; and when he would not go, but clung to them like one of those persistent Palestinian flies, bleating his parrot-cry of hunger with the same indifference to *"Imshi!"* ("Clear out!") that the flies show to an angry hand, they picked up clods to heave at him. But he dodged those, cursed the throwers as a matter or etiquette, and came back with the same persistence.

If the thirteenth man recognized him he gave no sign of it; and Suliman seemed to consider him not worth an effort, judging him with the beggar's rule in mind as a *maskin* (poor man) because he walked last. It would have been an insult to the rest and rank bad form, clods notwithstanding, to have begged from him before giving the men ahead first chance to show their quality.

So when he did at last approach Jim and cling to the skirt of his *abyi* nobody suspected old acquaintance. Jim told him gruffly to "*imshi*," like the rest of them, although one corner of his mouth quivered slightly in the faint beginnings of a smile. He might as well have tried to "*imshi*" the weather. Suliman clung on, and begged like an old hand at the game. The East believes in importunity and sets as high a value on reiteration as do the advertisers of the West.

The clod-throwing ceased because, unlike the curses that did not cease, one could not throw them any longer without hitting Jim. So Jim had to pause a minute to shake the persistent little nuisance off. And as most of the other twelve were shouting coarse obscenities, that gave him a chance to whisper without being overhead.

"Get away, you little bastard!" Then, in *sotto voce*—

"Where is Captain Catesby?"

"He is in sight. Oh, in the name of Allah—"

"Let Allah feed you! (*Follow me then.*) Go and scavenge. Go and steal. Am I God that I should feed you?"

Bleating piteously, and shedding tears that would have made the fabulous weeping crocodile look like a very poor actor indeed, Suliman turned aside to squat by the side of what had once been a cart-road but had grown to a mere track since bombardment wiped the village out. But he did not stay in that position much longer than was needed to be out of range of missiles.

* * * *

The normal daylight activity of camp and town was under way. Bugles were blowing. Guards had been relieved. Long strings of mules and horses were being led to water at the troughs. Engines were moving in the station yard, and strings of Egyptian laborers were slouching sullenly to work in the railroad sheds. Donkeys, women and other beasts of burden were emerging from the town, where the muezzin had long since finished wailing his injunction to the four winds.

One cartload of merchandise was already on its way from railway to town, and the kites were patrolling overhead on the watch for offal and remains. Suliman had a perfect right to head for the town, too, if he saw fit.

So had Catesby, looking like any other shiftless Arab mediating breakfast. He strolled along the cart track leisurely with his head down, imitating the measured native gait that looks so dignified but oftener than not means merely pride in laziness.

As he walked, fingering the pistol under his heavy brown cloak, he began wondering just how much the night's work had accomplished in the matter between Jenkins and himself. Adding it all up he could not make the total come to anything at all.

Suddenly he laughed, though. There was a hundred-piaster bank-note taken from a dead man! But Narayan Singh had found that, and if the real ownership should never be established no doubt it would be awarded to the Sikh. He took out the crumpled note and examined it, taking care to keep Suliman in sight.

He was not at all expert in Arabic, but presently he whistled, for he could spell out the thin, cramped, right-to-left writing when he took the time. An Arab writing with a fine pen can condense a deal of information on a half-sheet of ordinary notepaper.

The strip that fastened the halves of the note together was of generous proportions; it had been cut off with scissors, and looked like the lower third of a half-sheet. The gum used was very ordinary office paste, with the result that one corner had come loose and curled upward, betraying writing on both sides.

And because of the fact that Arabs write from right to left and, like some careless Westerners, reverse the sheet by turning it end over end, the name of the man to whom the document had originally been addressed and of the man who wrote it were both on the cut-off strip of paper. The fist name—that on the gummed side—was Brigadier-General Jenkins. The other name was "your honor's humble servant, Ibrahim Charkas."

Having spelled out the information, Catesby returned the note to his pocket and hurried forward, for Suliman was just entering the town street. He was not going to be fool enough to trust Suliman with the hundred piasters to pass along to Jim, having considerable less than Jim's high opinion of the boy. That was reciprocated.

Catesby's specialty was Sikhs. Being an Arab, Suliman's gift lay in personal devotion to whoever fed, clothed and favored him. It is not a bad gift, that personal loyalty, but there is nothing in it of the Sikh's wider idealism that attaches him to persons only because those persons stand for honorable service. Catesby lacked Jim's ability, which is wholly American, to ferret out the strong points of any breed whatever and play those sky-high.

The result was unfortunate. Suliman followed the party of thirteen to a small shed that stood beside a big one near the farther limit of the town. Into that they disappeared, donkey and all.

Suliman lurked in the doorway a hundred yards off, and Catesby watched him from a point of vantage behind the awning of a fruit-seller's shop. From where he stood he could read the name of the Zionist Commission on the door of the big shed.

At the end of about twenty minutes the donkey and the thirteen men emerged, Jim last again. The twelve went about their business separate ways, but Jim sat down to warm himself, Arab-fashion, in the early sun and lighted a cigarette.

When the last of the twelve was out of sight Suliman approached Jim with the beggar's whine again. They talked for about two minutes, and a coin changed hands for appearance's sake. Then Suliman came up-street to beg from Catesby. There was no one to overhear them—no need to beat about the bush.

"Jimgrim says you are to go back to Narayan Singh and tell him not to kill the *iblis*, who is in that place he is watching. He says you should stay with Narayan Singh, so that when Jimgrim wants you he can find you."

* * * *

Now if a Sikh had brought that message Catesby would have accepted it without demur. Moreover, he would have given that hundred-piaster note to a Sikh to give to Jim. But the eight-year-old Arab was different.

"Go back and say I have something for him. Ask him whether I shall go to him, or will he come to me. Say it's important."

"Give me whatever it is. He told me to come back to him."

"Do as I say."

There followed a considerable waste of time. Suliman did not dare to go running back with the message, knowing well enough that inquisitive observers might draw conclusions. He had the practical common sense to enter a shop and buy two native cigarettes "for the *khawaja* sitting yonder in the sun," as he was careful to explain.

The shopman was inquisitive, and had to be lied to *in extenso*, which took up more time. Finally Jim received the cigarettes and returned one to the messenger as gratuity. Thanks to Suliman there was nothing to call for comment.

But Jim had to sit and smoke the cigarette in order to complete the innocent picture, and it was several minutes before he strolled up the street to where Catesby waiting and went through the forms of pleased surprise and the lengthy Arab greeting of an unexpected friend. After that they strolled side by side, very slowly as befitted Arabs in the circumstances, and that entailed further delay.

Catesby gave him the hundred-piaster note. Jim examined it and whistled softly—a thing no Arab ever does; but the revelation startled him, and there was no one to overhear. Catesby explained briefly how he came by it; and then they went through the formula of leave-taking for the benefit of onlookers, which consumed another minute or two.

At last, however, Catesby went off alone to share Narayan Singh's vigil, and took his time on the way because no Arab ever hurries if that can possibly be helped. So it was twenty minutes more before he reached the deserted village and another five minutes after than before he discovered Narayan Singh.

The Sikh was lying in a dead man's tortured posture on the ground, and just beginning to recover consciousness. A stone the size of a coconut lay beside his head. It was ten more minutes before Catesby could get a word out of him.

"The door opened, *sahib*, and the *iblis* showed his head. I ordered him in again. He shut the door, and I watched it. A few minutes after that he showed himself over the top of the wall, and I, having orders not to shoot him, merely observed. Then he threw three stones at me, and the third one struck my head.

"How long ago did this happen? Soon after I left?"

"Nay. A long time after you left. I have been stunned—how should I know how long? But I think it happened just a very little while ago."

Catesby tried the door, but it was locked. So he set a charred beam against the wall and climbed, to peer in through the window. As far as he could seethe place was empty; and presently, scouting about, he found the imprints of two enormous naked feet in the dust. They were pointed away from the door, and he hardly could doubt they were those of the escaping *iblis*.

CHAPTER X

"Acting on information received."

All the ambitious men and women of history have come to grief finally by walking straight ahead into the same old simple trap. It is painted differently for different men, and the bait is big or little as the case may be. The goads that made them restless, so that they move when the trap is ready instead of staying still are pretty much the same in most cases; and, just as in the case of the tiger in his prime, there are usually jackals giving bad advice.

Jenkins was no exception. Taking advantage of the long-drawn interim between the armistice and the issuing of mandates, he had made of that camp at Ludd a very breeding-ground of politics.

As a fighter he had obtained distinction by stealing the credit for other men's successes for himself and by contriving to blame others for his failures. And he had no use for credit except as a means for making profit. So of course he had jackals tugging his heels impatiently, men who admired his disrespect for all the accepted rules of fair play and who would have outdone his methods if they had dared. One of them was Captain Aloysius Ticknor.

Ticknor likewise had ambitions, and was perfectly ready to sacrifice Jenkins at any moment for their attainment. But for the present Ticknor saw more immediate profit in working for his chief's advancement, like a man who rears a ladder to climb by, meaning to kick it down afterward or leave it leaning, just as suits him.

They were not in each other's secrets, because Jenkins never trusted anyone if he could help it. He preferred to make hints and innuendoes, on the strength of which a subordinate made good, then Jenkins got the credit; if the subordinate failed there was only one more victim on the long list of ruined youngsters "Jinks" had left behind him.

So Aloysius Ticknor, who would lose money to Jenkins at cards, for instance, and generally win it back with something added from junior subalterns, was exactly in the position of a jackal craving meat who did not know the tiger's real intentions although sure of the tiger's hunger. Jackal fashion he diagnosed the brigadier's nervous restlessness and offered the sort of advice he felt sure would be acceptable.

He was another pro-Arab, anti-Zionist, of course. You had to be that if you hoped to stay in Jenkins' good books for a minute.

"Why don't you send me into town, sir, to look things over."

"Might fall foul of the provost-marshal," Jenkins answered. "He's one of those stuffy bastards who resent what they call interference."

"If you show him up as incompetent by finding a cache of rifles under his very nose—" suggested Ticknor.

"Hm-m-m! Be a joke, wouldn't it? Not difficult either. The fool has his eye on Arabs all the time. There isn't an Arab store or dwelling that he hasn't searched. If the Arabs had one rifle hidden he'd have found it. He seems to think Jews are gentle angels who wouldn't do anything secretive if you paid them money for it."

"Suppose I look the Zionist quarters over, sir?"

"I'm not going to give you orders over the provost-marshal's head, if that's what you're driving at. If you can think of another excuse—"

"Oh, easily. You remember those three condemned huts? They're to be advertised for sale. I could go and inquire whether the Zionists would like to have them—promise nothing, of course, but offer to use influence."

"Yes, you might do that. But be sure you promise nothing. I shan't need you this morning. You can go for a stroll if you like," he added. "Buy yourself some souvenirs."

And he made a note in his diary there and then that he had given Ticknor personal leave of absence. He did it in pencil to be inked in later, so that he might change "personal" to "particular" if he should see fit.

So Captain Aloysius Ticknor, with nice red tables on his collar and the glow of astuteness radiating from him till he looked like light personified, started out with two dogs at his heels, swinging his service cane. Half an hour later, sweating rather more than he liked, because it offset his studied air of omniscient aloofness, he arrived in front of the Zionist store-shed on the far end of the town.

The door was locked, but a short, broad-shouldered, sweaty little Jew in black New York-made pants and a gray shirt was busy nailing scrap tin over a broken window-pane.

"Are you in charge here?" Ticknor asked him.

The Jew laid down the hammer and eyed his suspiciously. It was no more than hereditary mistrust of uniform because official-dom has always meant oppression for the Jew; but it was enough in itself to stir the lees of Ticknor's racial arrogance.

"Can't you answer? I asked, are you in charge here?"

"In charge of this hammer, yes. It is not my hammer. I make repairs—see?"

"Where's the key of the place?"

"I have it."

"Open the door then."

The Jew did not cringe, having left that uningratiating voice behind him in Moscow when he emigrated to America, but he obeyed with alacrity that might have disarmed Ticknor's suspicion. But Ticknor was feeling jubilant. He had come prepared to hide his real mission under a cloak of friendly interest and was naturally relieved to find that he could lay aside the hypocrisy. There might have been someone there who would have resented intrusion—some Zionist official on his dignity; and of all things in the world that he hated, he worst was having to be polite to people he disliked.

He walked straight into the great musty-smelling shed the instant the door opened, seeing in imagination a sort of pirates' stronghold piled full of contraband. But when his eyes grew used to the dim light he saw only very ordinary stores—spare hospital supplies, flour in barrels, clothing in bundles, tar, tools and calico in bales—extremely disappointing.

However, Jews are secretive and cunning. Doubtless there were rifles hidden in the bales—ammunition in the barrels. He nosed about all over the place, pushing things aside to see what lay behind or underneath them. Presently he found a bale that had been opened and wired up again.

"Come here, you!" he called. "Here, open this!"

The overstepped the limit of forbearance even of the individual in black pants. He came in, scratched the back of his head, rubbed his nose and went through the motions with his other hand suggestive of deference and blunt refusal that fought one with the other. A slight shrug of the shoulders indication absence of responsibility; but he said nothing.

"D'you hear me? Open it!"

"But why?"

The answer aroused suspicion to the danger-point. Where prejudice is strong judgment is always weak. Ticknor set to work to do the job himself, twisting at the wires with impatient fingers under the eyes of the bewildered Jew. He had got one wire undone when someone else darkened the doorway.

* * * *

"What is this?"

Ticknor turned impatiently to see a Jew of another type altogether watching him from the door through gold-rimmed pince-nez—the very man he did not want to meet that morning, but for whose benefit he had come prepared with the plausible excuse about the condemned huts. Aaronsohn was one of the intellectuals, a man of considerable private means, journalist and poet, who had thrown his whole fortune and energy into the Zionist movement.

Caught in the act of trespass without authority, and with dust clinging to the swear on his face and neck, he felt at a disadvantage that Aaronsohn appreciated fully. There seemed nothing for it but to bluff the thing through.

"Acting on information received," he said, "I am searching for stolen Government property."

"Acting on circumstantial evidence, I am now on my way to General Anthony to lodge a complaint against you," Aaronsohn answered with a grim smile. "But perhaps you have something in writing?"

"No need of it," Ticknor answered.

"No? We will see about that. Perhaps I had better see first what damage you have done."

"Perhaps you'd better open that bale and satisfy me what's inside it," sneered Ticknor.

Aaronsohn obliged him. And because the bale stood wedged between others, which made it awkward to unbind, he and the man in black pants dragged it out to the middle of the floor between them. There proved to be nothing in it but gray flannel shirts, each marked at the neck with the name of a New York manufacturer.

Aaronsohn chose to be sarcastic, twenty-five years' use of an acid pen having left that habit on the surface.

"I will leave you in charge of the plunder," he said, smiling with thin lips. "Stay here, and let me ask General Anthony to send you assistance."

Conscious of the strength of his position, and too old a hand at reprisals to waste invective on a man he could annihilate by much more concrete means, he walked straight out at that, leaving the door wide open.

Ticknor swore under his breath, reviewing his own position without getting any comfort from it. He knew he might depend on Jenkins to let him down completely, for he was under no delusion as to the brigadier's method of self-preservation.

It occurred to him presently that his one meager chance lay in still discovering what he came to find. It might be after all that Aaronsohn's indignation was a well-acted bluff.

What had brought the Jew there at that critical moment? What could possibly have brought him there but nervousness? What could have sent him hurrying off to Anthony but the hope of stopping the search before the secret was uncovered.

Thinking thus, his eye fell on the twelve square feet of floor where the bale had stood before they dragged it clear. He saw hinges—the butt-ends of long strap hinges passing under the next bale on the left.

"What's under the floor?" he demanded.

"Nothing," said the man in black pants.

"Drag that next bale away."

He helped him do it, and uncovered a trapdoor.

Hope ran ace-high again. He was the same alert, astute Aloysius Ticknor who had started forth that morning dreaming of high politics. Even his two dogs, sniffing for rats in a corner, seemed to appreciate the change, for they left their pressing business to come and wag their tails at him.

"Open her up!" he ordered.

Might as well be broke for burglary as trespass. Besides, all successful men take chances.

But the trapdoor would not raise. It was fastened down with one long nail driven in to the head. The man in black pants produced a crowbar from a corner and lent the strength of his stocky shoulders.

"I'll remember that in your favor," said Ticknor, not supposing that the Jew's readiness to help might be due to anything but the instinct of self-preservation.

Some men can convince themselves of anything they want to believe. Ticknor would have betted a year's pay that minute on there being loot under the floor, and another year's pay on top of that that both Aaronsohn and this man knew it.

So he was not surprised, he was merely elated and self-complacent when the nail came splintering out of the wood and the door creaked back at last. He did not stop to consider why the hinges should have yielded so reluctantly, or to study the rust on the ancient nail. There was too much down below to interest him—rifles, cartridges, revolvers, bayonets—the plunder of months from Ludd encampment!

That was a minute of triumph, worth ten times the sting of Aaronsohn's sarcastic insolence. Lord, wouldn't Jenkins be pleased! And think of Aaronsohn's chagrin! And the provost-marshal's, who had had his eye well wiped!

He jumped down into the cellar, struck a match and looked about him, but did not trouble to go as far as the end wall because there was hardly headroom and he had to stoop. Beside there might be snakes and vermin. So he did not notice a door at the end, communicating with the smaller shed next door, nor see the print of footsteps leading from it.

He climbed out again, sweating and dusty but almost busting with pleasure at his good luck. The Jew in black pants, peering down into the hole beside him, felt it incumbent to translate his thoughts into speech that might be understood.

"Well, I never! Those Arabs, mister, there is nothing they stop at! As a snake in the grass so is an Arab!"

"Lies about Arabs won't help you, my lad! You'd better stay here. Understand me?"

"Sure I stay here."

Ticknor laughed.

"You're a strange race. I never saw such perfectly acted conscious innocence. Talk of Chinamen—they're not in it with you."

He went to the door and looked up and down the street, hoping to catch sight of a soldier or policeman—anyone at all who might be sent to bring the provost-marshal's men; or better yet, sent running with a note to Jenkins.

There was no one in uniform in sight. He scribbled a note on the back of a private letter, replaced it in its envelope, readdressed it to the brigadier, contrived to seal it after a fashion by relicking the old gum, and beckoned a small boy who was sitting smoking outside a shop on the opposite side of the street fifty yards away.

Preferring not to advertise his find too widely for the moment, he judge it better to do his talking inside the building. So the small boy got a good view of the trapdoor, and a glimpse of what lay underneath.

"Listen. Do you know General Jenkins?"

The small boy nodded. There were few things he ever forgot, once he had rubbed acquaintance with them.

"Do you know how to find him?"

He nodded again.

"Take this letter to him, but don't show it to anybody else. If you come back quickly with an answer I'll give you five piasters."

The bribe was enormous. The small boy took the envelope and started off at a run. Ticknor returned to the trapdoor to gloat over his discovery and smoke a cigarette of triumph.

So again he missed something that might have given him thought. The boy stopped at the shop near which he had been sitting, and called through the open door.

"Oh, Jimgrim!"

A man in Arab costume came and stood in the shadow between the door-posts.

"Over there in the big shed there is a trapdoor. It is open. Underneath are rifles. An officer gave me this."

"Who is it for?"

"General Jenkins."

"All right. Run with it."

Suliman sat and pulled his boots off, for they were a concession to convention, not adjunct to speed. Stringing them around his neck by the laces he set off as fast as youth would let him.

Jimgrim turned back into the shop, smiling with tired eyes, to resume his conversation with a real Arab where it had broken off.

"Now, Ibrahim Charkas. Let's have that over again. No lies this time or I'll wring your neck.

CHAPTER XI

"There is money…take it and go away."

When Jim received the hundred-piaster note from Suliman he went at once into Mahommed Kaftar's coffee-shop and steamed it over the kettle until it fell into the original three pieces—two ragged halves and a strip of gummed paper. Then he drank coffee leisurely until the paper dried, turning it over on his knee and chuckling to himself.

"Mustn't say a word against Jenkins—um-m-m!"

Sir Henry Kettle's and General Anthony's injunction began to fit, still vaguely, into something suggestive of strategy based on information.

"Give a rascal rope enough and he's sure to hang himself."

But one must take precautions lest he trip too many others with the rope before the end comes. He made up his mind to see Ibrahim Charkas at once, not that there would be any obvious advantage to the community in saving that evasive rascal from the consequence of dallying with Jinks' spider web; but he did have instructions to discover who stole that TNT, and if one thing should lead to another, and that to Jinks' downfall, he would still be obeying orders.

Ibrahim Charkas ran one of those nondescript Arab stores in which everything was sold from sewing thread to tinned biscuits and souvenir photographs. He had even sold whisky until the provost-marshal interfered. Loss of the surreptitious liquor trade had cost him the custom of Sikhs and Gurkhas in addition to a staggering fine, so that business was not what it used to be and the stock in trade looked the part.

Dogged at a little distance by Suliman, who would not have traded his employment just then for a promise of paradise, Jim strolled up-street looking like an Arab whose wives were attending to business for him, lord of the earth and of leisure. There were plenty of other Arabs in the street and he had to be careful, but he watched his chance outside Charkas' shop to toss Suliman a coin in which to buy breakfast and tell him to wait until call. Then he went in ostensibly for cigarettes.

Charkas came out obsequiously from a little room in the rear to greet him, for the day was past when the store would support an assistant, except for a mere fetch-and-carry nonentity, who could hardly be trusted to sweep the place out least he steal whatever he could reach. Just then the nonentity was away on some kind of errand.

"*Shu bitrid, ya khawaja?*" ("What do you want, sir?")

Jim countered in English, and opened with his heaviest gun, laying down the two portions of the bank-note on a table at the back of the shop.

"Just take a look at those. When did you see them last?"

Charkas did not seem to know which to be surprised at more—the question or being addressed in English.

"Who are you that prefer a foreign language to your own?"

"None of your business! This is your business—this note— it's important—when did you see it last?"

"How should I know? I never saw it. I don't accept torn money."

"Look again. It was pasted together when you saw it last. I know where you had it from, but how did you get rid of it?"

"To whom should I pay a hundred piasters? Tee-hee-hee! Absurd! The business of this store is no longer that much in a week."

"Did you ever see this?" Jim asked him, turning over the strip of paper in both hands so as to show first the signature of Charkas on one side and then Jenkins' name on the other. "It came of the back of that note."

Charkas began to look like a cornered rat. The pupils of his eyes became pin-points, and narrow teeth showed prominently between his thin, parted lips. He made a quick motion with his hand, but Jim was quicker and seized him by both arms. Jim put his foot on it, and then picked up the strip of paper he had had to let fall.

"Better not try to make a hanging matter of it. Better use your head. It's fairly easy to make sense out of this writing. It's a letter from you to General Jenkins describing what certain men are doing, what they intend to do, and stating why you need more money. Jenkins gave you that hundred piasters. What did you do with it?"

There naturally flashed across Charkas' mind his recent interview with Jenkins, of which Jim knew nothing, any more that Jim knew that the man from whom the hundred-piaster note had been taken did not come by it from someone else, who in turn might have had it from a third man. Charkas decided that Jenkins must have betrayed him, more than making good the threat not come to his aid if needed. But he was still cautious.

"Who are you?" he asked again.

In strategy there is no sounder rule that to follow up one surprise with another one, the second if possible more unexpected than the first. The first one destroys confidence; the second promotes hysteria.

"I'm a man who found in Jerusalem the TNT that was stolen from the railway here."

Charkas turned to look about wildly for a weapon. Swift murder and sudden flight were all he could think of. He looked twice longingly toward a desk in the dingy back office.

"Come in here," he said mysteriously.

Jim kicked the knife into the corner and followed him so quickly that he reached the desk abreast of him. Their hands closed on the lid simultaneously. Jim's right hand forced Charkas into a chair. With his left he raised the lid.

"Thought so!"

"There was a revolver and a dagger with a wavy edge.

"Which would you have used? Um-m-m! I guess you're scared enough to have fired and alarmed the town. Let's see what else is in here—sit still, now! Don't move or I'll get a rope out of the store and tie you."

He put his foot on the Arab's lap to keep him from bolting while he searched through a litter of papers at random. They were mostly bills, receipts and private letters. Nothing of obvious importance.

"There is money at the back," said Charkas. "Take it and go away."

Jim whistled. Charkas shuddered. There is nothing in the world some Arabs hate so much as that. They say only the devil whistles. One can never know beforehand for certain, of course, but Charkas was hardly the kind of man one would expect to believe in that superstition.

Adding the shudder to the offer of the bribe; Jim drew a false conclusion that led nevertheless to discovery. Supposing that Charkas' anxiety was for the papers in the desk, he went on searching; whereas the man actually was past fear on that account, thinking now of nothing but how to escape; and his nerves were in such a state that the whistle tortured him.

Jim found the money, glanced at it and tossed it aside. Then he turned over the papers again, stacking them one on top of the other, and presently whistled again.

"What in thunder did you keep this for?" he asked, removing his foot from Charkas' lap as he turned his back to the desk and laughed. "Are you the ringleader of thieves here, and keep the proof of it to show like a Government certificate?"

Suddenly a fragment of Charkas' native wit returned and he remembered why he had kept it.

"That is the memorandum informing General Jenkins that two tons of TNT were in a truck in the siding."

"So I see. Well?"

"General Jenkins gave it to me—into my hand!"

If Jenkins proposed to betray her, then two could play at that game. All the bitterness and venom that the Arab min inherited from Ishmael and cultivated under Turkish rule came to the surface. Revenge looked sweeter at that minute than safety. Thoughts of flight vanished.

"General Jenkins gave me that hundred-piaster note. He has given me other sums from time to time. I will swear to it in court. He has been paying me to organize the thieving."

"Why?"

"In order to blame it on the Zionists. He hates Zionists. He is pro-Arab."

"And he gave you that memorandum so that you could steal the TNT?"

"So that my men could steal it, yes."

Jim tried not to look incredulous. It would take more than Charkas' word to convince him that Jenkins would be such a fool as that.

"When did he give it to you?"

"On the third, I think it was. Yes, on the evening of the third."

"At what time?"

"Five o'clock."

"Are you sure?"

"Yes, because I met the afternoon train and walked up to his office afterwards."

"This is dated the third at four o'clock. He could only have just received it. Was he in the office when you went there?"

"He reached it just ahead of me. The messenger brought the note; he signed for it, read it, and handed it to me."

Jim laughed.

"You mean he turned away and you stole it off his desk—now don't you?"

Charkas denied that hotly—swore by the God of his fathers and by Mohammed and all the saints in paradise that Jenkins had given him the paper. But that was too obviously stupidly untrue. A blundering, fatuous schemer Jenkins might be, but not such a simpleton as that. There was proof on that slip of paper in Jim's pocket that Jenkins had known a lot about the thieving—probably proof enough to ruin him; but Jim's task was to let the brigadier ruin himself. In all likelihood Anthony would refuse to listen if he should come with the blackest proof imaginable.

"Look here," he said, "you're all in—d'you realize it? You've only got one chance—king's evidence. Come across with a clean story and I'll do my best for you."

The rat instinct for sudden flight crossed the Arab's mind again. He rolled his eyes toward the door secretively, but Jim saw that and put his foot back on the man's lap.

"Stay put!" he laughed, shoving him once or twice hard in the stomach. "Come on, spill the story. Who's the *iblis*?"

Charkas looked relieved. He even chuckled.

"He is an Egyptian. I do not know his name, but he is a great charlatan, who left Egypt because of the police. Now he is very much disturbed—tee-hee-hee! He is expert at encouraging thieves. He gives them magic against bullets—tee-hee-hee!—and he demands two-thirds of all the plunder in return.

"But he cannot dispose of his share of the plunder without assistance; and he does not know where the men who come for it have hidden it. Tee-hee! He is very much exercised."

"I happen to know where they have hidden it," said Jim.

Charkas snickered scornfully.

"I don't believe you. How could you know?"

"I was with the *iblis* most of last night, and I went with the men who came at dawn to hide the stuff away. The *iblis* is waiting for me now to come back and tell him where they hid it."

Charkas threw his hands up in despair.

"You must be a bigger devil than the *iblis* himself!"

"Maybe. We'll discuss that later if you like. The point is, are you going to come across, or would you rather I'd arrest you now and take you straight to Jenkins?"

"What do you want of me?"

"The names of all your men. Here's a pencil. Here's paper. Write them down."

Charkas hesitated for a moment, then tried to wet the pencil on his dry lips and obeyed him.

"I will make a full confession because you have promised I shall escape imprisonment by doing so."

Jim laughed again.

"I dare say your sentence will be cut in half," he answered. "That's the best you can hope for. You can withdraw all you've said if you like, plead not guilty and take the consequences."

"No, no, no! I will confess and plead guilty."

It was at this point that Suliman called out through the doorway and Jim went out to speak with him, first pocketing the Arab's dagger and revolver, but forgetting the knife he had kicked into a corner. Charkas had not forgotten it, but when Jim returned to the inner office he was back in the chair again.

"Here is the list of names," he said, offering the sheet of paper.

Jim started to read it. All the light there was came through the office door and a dusty glass window set in the partition. He turned to let the light fall on the paper, and suddenly sprang backward.

The knife missed his stomach by a fraction of an inch. The blow was so savage that Charkas could not check it; his fist swung three-quarters of a circle and drove the knife nearly to the hilt into the wall behind.

"Nice sort of scorpion, aren't you! Leave the knife sticking there. Now sit back and tell me your story all over from the beginning."

This time Charkas was really convinced of helplessness, and beyond that he lied about everybody else and tried to present himself as a more or less innocent weakling involved in crime unwillingly by Jenkins, told a moderately truthful tale.

By the time he had finished the brigadier himself came clattering down-street on horseback, jubilant at the news of Ticknor's discovery. Ten minutes of so later a platoon of British Tommies marched up, sweating freely, and took charge of the Zionist store-shed. Jenkins rode away again, red-faced with triumph, and Ticknor followed him on foot.

It was not ten minutes after that when Catesby came hurrying in search of Jim. He had shed his disguise and was back in uniform; and he had overtaken Suliman, who was returning tired and breathless for his five piasters from Ticknor. Suliman pointed out the shop door and followed Ticknor back again up-street.

"What's new?" asked Jim.

"Bad news for you. The *iblis* pretty nearly brained Narayan Singh with a piece of coping-stone, and scooted God knows where. I had to take Narayan Singh back to camp to have his head dressed, and the doctor ordered him to bed. What are you looking happy about?"

"The prospect of breakfast and sleep. Did you see Jinks?"

"Yes, looking as pompously pleased as a ripe tomato. The brute didn't acknowledge my salute."

"Never mind. Jinks is his sure-enough name, old man. You'll be out from under arrest almost before you know it. Too bad about the *iblis*, but we'll get him yet. Meanwhile, there's this critter.

"Now you understand, Charkas, this officer is going to stay here and watch you until the provost-marshal's men come, and you'll go with them under arrest. Take my advice and say nothing. Don't talk to anyone. Don't answer questions.

"Let General Jenkins say what he pleases and do what he pleases. Hold your tongue until you see me again. So long, Catesby."

He left the shop and strolled up-street toward the camp as leisurely as if the heritage of all Allah were sleeping in his veins. Presently Suliman tagged along after him, grinning with contentment for a five-piaster note.

CHAPTER XII

"Good sunny night to you! Sweet dreams!"

Having faced the *iblis* in the dark and slept at frequent intervals afterward, Suliman considered the lid on gambling lifted and set forth to stake the five piasters against the capital of certain small boys of the lines, in a mysterious card game that did not call for a complete pack, and of which only he knew the rules.

Jim got into uniform, found the provost-marshal and then went straight to Jenkins' office. The brigadier was radiant and red-faced in the center of flattering juniors, pouting his lips as he made little of the morning's work.

"Very simple. Obvious to anyone with eyes in his head. I gave Ticknor his instructions, and there you are. Oh, hullo, Grim: Wiped your eyes for you. Didn't need you after all. I told you we'd find Zionists at the bottom of this. What have you been doing?"

"Very little, I'm afraid. I arrested Ibrahim Charkas, though, this morning. Left him in charge of Captain Catesby until the provost's men could come and get him."

Jenkins changed colors, flushing redder than ever, so that his ears and the back of his neck resembled rare roast beef.

"Catesby is under arrest himself," he snapped.

"His parole was lifted, sir, to give him opportunity to gather evidence in his own case."

"I know that. It was my doing. I wanted to give him every chance. I signed the order releasing him; but that doesn't give him authority to arrest people and hold prisoners. I shall have to look into this."

Jim hoped he would look into it, and held his tongue. Jenkins began to grow more obviously nervous every minute. The flatterers only irritated now, and he turned on them savagely.

"What are we all loafing here for? Is there nothing to do—no orders? You wait here a minute, Major Grim; I want to speak with you."

The juniors remembered urgent business suddenly, and left in different directions. Jenkins, jerking at his buffalo-horn mustache, turned and faced Jim.

"What did you arrest Charkas for?"

"On his own confession of his part in stealing the TNT."

"Um-m-m!"

The brigadier paced up and down the narrow room.

"What did he say?"

"That this is a full list of the thieves he has been employing."

Jenkins seized the sheet of paper.

"Excellent! Excellent! We can seize all these men and they'll be implicating one another within ten minutes. But you ought to have brought Charkas here to me before the provost interviews him. If this list is correct Charkas ought to be treated as a king's witness and released after the trail. However, I'll send this list to the provost with my compliments; it'll make him wince. Did you get the *iblis*?"

"No."

"Pouff!" sneered Jenkins.

Jim deliberately fed the fires of scorn, judging the man nicely.

"I thought I'd get some sleep, sir, and then go after him again."

"Sleep! Sleep! 'Pon my soul! Is that an American habit, to sleep while your hunted man runs? All right, go to sleep then! I'll attend to the rest of this myself. Good sunny night to you! Sweet dreams!"

But Jim did not sleep yet a while. He went first to Narayan Singh in the great hot hospital marquee. The Sikh was fretting in impotent fury at being out of action, lying down because that had been ordered, but tossing like a fritter on a pan.

"I am all right, *sahib*. My head hurts, but that is nothing. I was stunned for a few minutes by a stone from the paw of that black ape that calls himself an *iblis*; but it would take ten such stones all striking in the same place to make me give up the hunt. Catesby sahib, who is a precaution-*wallah*, ordered me in there and I obeyed.

"You let me out again, Jimgrim *sahib*, and turn me loose with a rifle and bayonet. I will bring back that *iblis* for you like a beetle on a pin."

Jim had seen the doctor's memorandum of the case.

"Do you want to go after him?"

"When was I ever chicken-hearted, Jimgrim *sahib*, that you ask me that?"

"All right, go to sleep them. When it stands written on your report card that you've had five hours' sleep I'll fetch you out of here and we'll see."

The Sikh promptly shut his eyes and lay down flat on the cot. But Jim had hardly turned his back before he signaled the Jat orderly.

"Oh, brother," he said, "the doctor *sahib* will ask if I have slept, in order to write the report of it on a card. You know what the answer will be?"

"Always from me a truthful answer. So and so long you were sleeping—so and so long restless—so and so long talkative—so and so many drinks of water—temperature this and that. I am seeking promotion."

"Ah! Do they promote cripples, these *dakitars*?"

"Nay. A man needs strength to lift great carcasses like thine."

"If that *dakitar* learns I have not slept for five hours straight on end, you will be an orderly too badly crippled for promotion. This is my word. I have said it—I, Narayan Singh."

The orderly returned to his stool by the door, grumbling about the trails of a man who seeks to rise in his profession, and Narayan Singh, with his mind at least quite relieved, dropped off into the land of dreams, from which he was awakened at intervals by the sound of Suliman's voice behind the tent quarreling with two other urchins about the ever changing rules of chance.

At the end of an hour or two, when all the money in sight had found its way into Suliman's pocket, the three boys sat back against the tent to smoke stale cigar butts and gossip. It was in that way that Narayan Singh picked up some information that he put to good use later on.

* * * *

Jim meanwhile met Catesby coming into camp ahead of Ibrahim Charkas, who was in charge of the provost's men.

"There's one thing for you to do now," he said. "Get conclusive proof of where you were on the afternoon of the third between four and five o'clock. The buffalo is going to blunder. I can see it coming."

"That's easy."

"Get your proof then, and keep it absolutely to yourself."

Jim still had one small errand before he could go to sleep himself. He went to General Anthony's marquee, and found to his delight that Jenkins was there ahead of him. The Zionist-journalist Aaronsohn was in there too, looking horribly uncomfortable in a thin-lipped, calm and collected way. Jenkins was still holding forth.

"The evidence is all in. I've asked the provost-marshal to exert himself in rounding up that list of Charkas' men. Charkas himself will swear that he was paid by the Zionists to steal rifles for them. The rifles were found in the Zionists' store. What more do you want?"

General Anthony uncrossed his legs and recrossed them, tapping on his desk with a pencil. He said nothing—not at all a rare habit of his.

"I've one thing more to add," said Jenkins. "I saw Charkas fifteen minutes ago. He tells me Major Grim has found the original memorandum from the R.T.O to me about the TNT that was stolen—found it in Charkas' desk. Charkas proposes to turn king's witness, and he vows he had the memorandum from Captain Catesby, to whom he paid money for it."

Anthony looked visible distressed. Jim tried hard to do the same.

"Don't you think we'd better cancel that parole altogether and order Catesby under close arrest?" said Jenkins stiffly.

Butter would not have melted in his mouth. You could tell at a glance how he hated to be mixed up, even in a judicial way, with such abominable misconduct in an officer.

"Yes," said Anthony. "Yes, yes, I'm afraid so."

He took pen and paper.

"One moment, sir," Jim interposed. "May I ask a question?"

"Fire away, Grim."

"Not you, sir; General Jenkins."

"Well?"

There was fire in Jinks' eyes, by way of reminder that he who can break captains can break majors just as easily. But Jim's first words disarmed suspicion.

"About Charkas. He told me a long-winded story. I didn't write it down, but from memory I should say it bears out certain points of which you've just said."

Jenkins almost purred aloud. This was the handsome way to make amends. He there and then forgave Jim even that left-handed apology on the railway-station platform.

"Charkas told me among other things how he came to know about the existence of that railway memorandum. If what he said is true it may help cinch the case.

"He says you were down on the afternoon of the third; that he followed you up, because he wanted to ask some sort of favor; that you and he reached your office at about the same time; and that he saw you receive and open the memorandum. He says you laid it down for a minute, but he didn't have time to more than glance at it. So he formed the idea of getting hold of it somehow in order to learn the exact details. Does that correspond with your recollection of that afternoon?"

"Yes, I think it does. Yes, I did meet the train that day. Yes, I remember Charkas came to the office to bother me about something."

"About five o'clock, he said."

"Must have been almost exactly five o'clock."

Anthony began scribbling on a pad.

"Are you definite on that point, General Jenkins?"

"Certainly. My memory's exact. Charkas must have gone straight to Catesby and got the memorandum from him, because

I gave Catesby his orders—as I explained at the time when the theft was discovered—within twenty minutes of receiving the memorandum."

Anthony drew out a file of papers from a drawer of his desk, and turned them over slowly.

"I see you say in your original complaint against Catesby—made while I was away in Egypt—that you were not sure of the exact time when you gave him the memorandum and orders to take over the TNT."

"I remember now, though. Grim's question brought the facts to mind."

"You're ready to swear to it now at the court martial?"

"Certainly."

"Very well. Have Catesby rearrested. Is there anything else, Grim?"

"The *iblis*, sir. I interviewed him last night."

"The deuce you did!"

"I've evidence enough against him to call for his arrest on military grounds."

"All right. I'll sign a warrant. Do you know where he is?"

"Not at the moment."

"Are you sure we can convict him?"

"Perfectly."

Without more ado Anthony began to fill out a regulation form.

"Better describe him as 'a person unknown—colored—believed to be a leper—accused of plotting to loot the military camp.' There."

He handed it to Jim. The printed portion was couched in the customary legal verbiage intended to convey the meaning without too formal crudity, that the prisoner should be caught, brought in and delivered alive or dead.

Jim put it in his pocket and went to his tent to sleep until late afternoon. Brigadier-General Jenkins, on the other hand, after restating his opinion of the Zionists for Aaronsohn's benefit, marched down to the place where they confined civilian prisoners, to see Charkas alone and drill him on his part. A very cautious, forehanded brigadier was Albert Jenkins, although given to expressing triumph rather sooner than was wise.

He had the ill taste to laugh aloud on his way back, as he passed Catesby in his tent, this time with two armed sentries standing on guard in front of it.

CHAPTER XIII

"The chain's complete."

It was growing dark when Jim emerged from his tent feeling less at ease than he cared to admit to himself. A note had come from Catesby, who was now to all intents and purposes incommunicado, to the effect that from five until six on the evening of the third he had been inquiring, at Jenkins' verbal request, into an accident that had taken place several days previously. A civilian had had his leg broken by a gun-wheel, and civilian witnesses had been difficult to find; but he had unearthed one, and was questioning him at the time when Jenkins pretended he had given the order about the TNT. Now he could not find the man again to prove the fact.

Jim had the note in his hand. As Catesby's next friend he had the right to visit him in any circumstances, just as a lawyer may go to his client in jail.

Things looked pretty bad at the moment. Bull-buffalo Jenkins was caught in a net of lies, certainly; but like many another buffalo before him he was going to be able to blunder out of it by brute force unless the unexpected happened. But it always does.

There seems to be a natural law that when chicanery has reached a certain stage of ripeness, and the elements of decency begin to rebel, all the clues required to link the crimes with the criminal appear on the surface one by one, almost exactly as when two chemicals are mixed and one of them disintegrates. Examination of the career of any criminal or of any public scandal will confirm the phenomenon.

It is easy to talk airily of luck and coincidence. Luck is an element of crime and loose thinking. The fact is that honest persistency sets natural laws to working, with the result, for instance, that an inventor on the trail of one idea discovers an entirely different one that he never dreamed of; a general, wholly bent on a definite, ably worked-out line of strategy discovers an unexpected flaw in the enemy's design that he would have missed if his own arrangements had been careless. There is no luck about it. It is law.

So, although Jim was surprised and rather annoyed at the moment, he stumbled that minute on a clue. Aaronsohn, the vitriolic journalist in gold-rimmed glasses, was sitting outside the tent on a camp-stool, a hand on either knee in an attitude of suppressed impatience. He got to his feet the instant Jim appeared.

"You are Major Grim, I think. I would like to talk to you."

"I'm in a hurry," Jim warned him.

"I am not. Why not do your errand and I will wait here for you? I have waited already two hours. You were asleep and I did not care to disturb you."

"Something important, eh?"

"To me, yes. To you, perhaps not."

"All right. Wait in my tent. Help yourself to cigarettes, and I'll be right back."

Instead of going to Catesby as he had intended, Jim went straight to the hospital tent, where he found Narayan Singh sitting at the end of the cot in glowering impatience.

"Have you slept?" he asked him.

"Ask the orderly, *sahib*."

Jim beckoned the orderly and put the question.

"Hah! Never was such a sleeper! He has snored so for five hours on end that the very tent-poles shook, and I had to wake him twice lest the other patients get out of bed to murder him."

Jim laughed and went to find the doctor.

"Is Narayan Singh fit to be discharged?" he asked.

"No, but I'll discharge him like a shot. Most Sikhs enjoy a short spell in hospital, but that man has more excuses for discharging him than a porcupine has bristles. He's an interesting specimen, and not badly hurt; three days would see him as right as a trivet. I've talked with him on and off for about three hours just for the fun of it."

"Hasn't he slept at all?"

"Not much. But you know what Sikhs are; they can go without sleep for a tremendous time, and make it up afterwards. The last excuse he tried on me was a story that his father died of hydrophobia because he couldn't stand hospital environment at night, and he suggested the disease might be hereditary.

"Sure, I'll let him out—a liar like that deserves anything. Tell him to come back and have his head dressed again after he has seen the lady."

Outside between the tents Jim gave Narayan Singh his warrant to arrest the *iblis*.

"Have you any idea where to look for him?" he asked.

"Surely, *sahib*. That Suliman played a game with other young sprouts of wickedness outside the place where I lay. Afterwards they talked until Suliman grew sleepy and went off with all their money.

"They told the gossip of the lines: how certain men had seen the *iblis* cross the railway line this morning, but were afraid to interfere with him. He was heading due east. I think, *sahib*, he will dance again tonight to summon thieves and learn from them how much has happened. If he does—!"

"You'd better take some men with you."

"Aye, *sahib*—four men if I may choose them."

"Will you go in disguise?"

"Not I! We will take rifles with bayonets, wear our uniforms and bring back that *iblis* in the name of a Sikh, whose head is no proper target for roof-stones. There is honor involved."

"All right."

Jim made arrangements for Narayan Singh to have the selection of four volunteers, and got written permits for them all to leave camp after dark. Then he returned to Aaronsohn.

* * * *

The Zionist had lit the lamp and was reading a Hebrew magazine in Jim's chair with that peculiar manner of armed intensity that characterizes the thinkers of the movement. His Vandyke beard and thin, Semitic nose, and a narrow shawl thrown loosely over his shoulders, made him look in that uncertain light like one of the statesmen-priests who used to intrigue in medieval history.

"Now I'm at your service."

"I have come to appeal to you as a fellow American, Major Grim."

"Don't forget I'm in British uniform."

"I am also an American, as it were in service under British rules and regulations."

"The positions seem different to me. However—"

"You are the only American in British uniform to whom I can appeal. I am not under arrest for the present. They have spared me that indignity, although I understand that General Jenkins demanded it.

"I am charged with plotting to steal British rifles, and with hiding them under the floor of our store-shed, where they were discovered this morning by a Captain Ticknor. Now I know nothing about those rifles. We have never used that space beneath the floor. We only hire the place.

"I have no notion how the rifles got there; how should I have? I am only quite sure that no Zionist had a hand in it, for I know what every Zionist in Ludd has been doing all the time. But how can I prove it?

"I am told you exposed a plot against Zionists in Jerusalem. Will you help us now?"

Jim sat down on the bed and smiled. Aaronsohn took the smile for mere politeness covering hesitation, and turned loose all his persuasive power.

"Whatever your racial prejudices, Major Grim, the predicament we Zionist are placed in surely must appeal to you. On the one hand the British Government promises us everything—a national home for Jews in Palestine—assistance—fair play; and some of their officers try to make good that promise. I give them full credit. They haven't much intelligence from our point of view, but they act according to their lights.

"On the other hand some of the officers, General Jenkins among them, stop at nothing to put us in a bad light, and do everything within their power to handicap us in every way. Such men have even less intelligence than the others, but their official position gives them opportunity."

"The British are not all fools," said Jim.

"That is after all a matte of opinion. Certainly some of them are just according to their lights; but it is the very sense of justice that I dread in this instance.

"General Anthony will order a court martial on me and a handful of others. All the officers who are anti-Zionist will exert themselves to discover circumstantial evidence against us. We have none whatever—"

"Oh, yes, you have," said Jim.

"But what? I have been allowed to visit the place since the discovery, and it is true that it can be shown that the rifles were carried in through a door connecting with a place next door that is own by Arabs.

"But they will answer, 'What does that prove?' Only that we paid Arabs to do the stealing for us! I am told that Ibrahim Char-kas, who is the worst kind of criminal, will swear that we Zionist paid him."

"Don't worry about that," said Jim. "I think I know enough to prick that bubble. I'll provide you with some evidence when the time comes."

"But what? What do you know? Tell me—I insist."

"It 'ud take too long," said Jim. "Besides, the value of what I know largely depends on my discovering something else that seems to have nothing to do with it. I'm interested in that just now. I'm at my wits' end, and want time to think."

"Let me try to help you. We will help each other."

"You can't help."

"How do you know? State the case and try me."

"I must find an Arab named Sayed Haurani, who was talking to Captain Catesby by halfway between the station and the town on the afternoon of the third between five and six o'clock. I need him in a hurry."

Aaronsohn looked startled.

"I suppose you have orders to gather further evidence against Zionists?" he asked acidly.

"No."

It was Jim's turn to sit up and take notice.

"Is Sayed Haurani a Zionist? Of course he isn't. But what d'you know of him?"

"Why do you want to know?"

"To save Captain Catesby from being cashiered on a false charge."

"Sayre Haurani was my messenger. I dismissed him on that occasion for returning an hour late from the station, because I disbelieved his story."

Jim lay back on the bed and threw his legs in the air.

"Can you find him?" he asked.

"Certainly."

"Tonight?"

"Yes."

"The chain's complete! Go and find him. Produce him at eight o'clock tomorrow morning in General Anthony's office and the world's your oyster!"

"I have no desire to eat a world on the half-shell, Major Grim."

"You shall have Jenkins' head on a slaver!"

"Pardon me, I am not Salome."

"What in thunder could a man want more than that? Go on, Aaronsohn—find your man! Produce him at eight A.M. and leave the rest to me."

In vain Aaronsohn coaxed, cajoled and persuaded. Jim shut up like a clam; but his eyes betrayed such infinite enjoyment that even Aaronsohn at last took comfort from it and went away to find the discharged messenger.

* * * *

The minute he was gone, Jim went over to Catesby's tent and called out to him, standing between the sentries rather that run the risk of stirring Jenkins any further by being seen entering the tent.

"All right, old son, you're cleared. Be at headquarters at eight o'clock. They'll fetch you anyhow."

"What's happened?"

"Good news, that's all. Go to sleep and dream about promotion."

From there we went straight to General Anthony, who looked worried. He called Jim into an inner room and shut the door.

"What's at the bottom of all this, Grim? Have you any idea?

"It looks to me as if Jenkins is going to get away with murder once again. He has got the whole camp by the ears. We shall have the provost-marshal sending in his resignation next. After that I suppose there'll be a decoration sent out from home for me to pin on Jenkins! Damn it, the man's luck in unbelievable!"

Jim put his tongue in his cheek.

"I've not a word to say against him, sir!"

"What have you come here for, then?"

"Merely to suggest that if you think both cases are sufficiently important you might order a preliminary hearing first thing to-morrow morning—all witnesses to be present as a matter of fair play."

"Why? Have you got something?"

"I'd like to see Jenkins given an early chance to take all the credit to himself. Maybe he deserves it," Jim answered.

"Oh! Very well. By gad, Grim, if you let Jenkins get away with this I'll have you sent back to America. You think Catesby ought to have a hearing too tomorrow morning, eh?"

"He ought to come first, sir."

"Yes, he has the right to that. What else?"

"Nothing else. If you'll issue the necessary orders, sir, I know of nothing that need spoil your appetite for dinner or your sleep tonight."

"That so? Ahem! Somebody blundered, eh?"

"Good night, sir."

CHAPTER XIV

"Proceed with the case."

Next morning the office at G.H.Q. was crowded, for the provost-marshal was there with all his prisoners; and there were a score of witnesses in addition, to say nothing of Brigadier Jenkins in his glory, and Aaronsohn, who was halfway between prisoner and witness. The latter had a nondescript, rebellious-looking Arab beside him, who had had to be bribed to come at all.

Catesby was sitting in a corner by himself, in theoretical charge of two sentries, who stayed outside the office door.

Anthony came in punctual to the second.

"Major Grim here?"

To Jenkins' fidgety disgust Jim was busy talking to Charkas over against the wall.

"I think he's too busy interfering with witnesses to answer his name," snapped the brigadier.

"Major Grim!"

"Yes, sir."

"What are you doing over there?"

"Cautioning a prisoner to tell the truth for his own sake."

"Ahem! I understand you appear for Captain Catesby? You want the case heard?"

"If you please."

"I object to that," said Jenkins. "Captain Catesby is an important witness in the next case."

"I will invite comment from you at the proper time, general," said Anthony without looking up. "Call the prisoner."

Catesby marched up and faced the desk.

"Then I want the room cleared," Jenkins blustered.

"I want all my witnesses, including Charkas, in the room for the present," Jim said quietly.

"I particularly want Charkas out of the room," insisted Jenkins. "He has got nothing to do with this case."

"Has he?" asked Anthony.

"Yes, sir," answered Jim.

"The defense is within its rights," said Anthony.

And Jenkins, not exactly knowing why, but intuitively sensing disaster, turned about three shaded redder in the face.

"I'm ready to hear what you have to say, general," Anthony announced; and Jenkins opened fire on the unhappy Catesby, charging him first with culpable neglect and disobedience to orders in permitting two tons of TNT to be stolen from a truck, and secondly with felony in having given the railway memorandum to Charkas, enabling him to steal the stuff.

Also with being an accessory to a felony before and after the fact, and with conduct in general unbecoming to an officer and a gentleman.

At that point Jim produced the railway memorandum and laid it on the table.

"In case of need I may ask to have it examined for fingerprints," he said. "I expect to be able to prove that those of Captain Catesby are not on it, whereas those of General Jenkins and Ibrahim Charkas are. But that may not be necessary."

"Are you making any implication?" demanded Jenkins.

"No, sir."

"Proceed with the case," commanded Anthony.

Jenkins had a peroration all prepared; he was constitutionally incapable of doing anything without calling attention to his own virtues, and he dissertated at length on the high calling of an officer until Anthony cut him short and demanded evidence.

Jenkins bit his mustache, and swore under his breath.

"My charge in itself is evidence," he said, "sufficient evidence to hold the prisoner. I am withholding my chief witness for the next case."

"You mean that you appear as prosecutor and witness?" asked Anthony.

"Yes—on the charge of culpable negligence."

"I'm willing that charge should be taken first by itself," said Jim, and Jenkins looked vastly relieved and nodded to him.

"Go on oath if you're a witness," ordered Anthony, and Jenkins duly kissed the well-worn Testament.

"Now go ahead. I'll write down your evidence."

* * * *

Jenkins described then in great detail as to his own feelings in the matter, but vaguely as to time, how he had given orders to Catesby on the evening of the third to go and take charge of the TNT, which was subsequently stolen and recovered in Jerusalem.

"And I ask," he said, "that the prisoner be held for court martial on this charge, and that the other charges be taken tomorrow."

"Certainly not," said Anthony. "Any questions, Major Grim?"

Jim pinned Jenkins down to giving the exact time—first, however, getting him to boast about his excellent memory. Driven to it, Jenkins swore on oath that he had given the memorandum to Catesby shortly after five o'clock in the afternoon of the third.

"You gave it into his hand?"

"Yes."

"You swear to that?"

"Certainly."

Jim put up Catesby, who told a perfectly straight story of having questioned a man named Sayed Haurani for an hour, beginning before five o'clock, at a point more than a mile away from Jenkins' office, and by Jenkins' orders on that date.

Jenkins reserved cross-examination. With his eye on Charkas, whose face was the picture of indecision and mixed emotions, Jim called Sayed Haurani. The man identified Catesby and confirmed his story in all particulars.

Jenkins tried to break down the story by bullying the witness, but failed. The man was insolently confident.

"I ask to have the hearing postponed until I can look up this man's antecedents," said Jenkins. "He's an obvious liar. This is what comes of turning an accused officer loose to suborn evidence in the bazaar."

Anthony waved the objection aside, and Jenkins grew still more uncomfortable.

"Either this witness is committing perjury, or I did," he blustered. "It's no joking matter."

"Obviously," said Anthony, again without looking up. "Call your next witness if you have one, Major Grim."

Then Aaronsohn stood up before the desk and confirmed Sayed Haurani's evidence, explaining how he had disbelieved the man at the time and had dismissed him for returning from the station late. He gave the Arab a high character for everything except discipline, describing him as an insolently disobedient man, who did not trouble himself to lie about things as a rule, but shook off rebuke with an air of bold indifference.

At last Anthony began to look very hard at Jenkins, who avoided his gaze by pretending to look about the room for someone who was not there. Jim had his eye on Charkas. A great deal depended now on the effect that what had gone before had had on Charkas.

"Perhaps you'd like to re-examine General Jenkins yourself sir?" he asked Anthony.

Anthony took the cue, and grilled the brigadier on each point of his evidence, reducing him at last to a state of boiling anger bordering on insubordination.

"If I'm charged with lying on oath I'd like to know it," he snapped.

"Stand down, sir," ordered Anthony.

"Ibrahim Charkas," ordered Jim.

He met Charkas' eye and glanced meaningly at Jenkins, but there was no need. The Arab had seen which was the cat was jumping, and decided there was more profit for himself in contributing to Jenkins' downfall than in trying to support him.

He could not tell the truth, of course; that would have been too much to expect of him. But he blurted out the whole story of the plot to ruin the Zionists, and accused Jenkins of having not only suggested it but of having paid for it as well. And instead of admitting the theft of the TNT memorandum, he accused Jenkins of having given it to him.

* * * *

That was enough for that morning. It was only a preliminary hearing, not a court martial.

Anthony decided to postpone the hearing of the case against Charkas and the other thieves. He dismissed charges against Catesby, entering against them the two words "honorably discharged" for future reference. The two soldiers who had stood guard over Catesby were then formally transferred to "Jinks," who marched off to his own tent a prisoner.

Anthony had turned to Aaronsohn to tell him that pending the trial of the thieves there would be no restraint on his movements or implication against him, when there was a disturbance at the door. A sentry came to explain.

"Admit him," said Anthony, and in marched Narayan Singh, with his uniform in shreds and the marks of a strenuous fight all over him.

He was bleeding slightly in one or two places, and one eye was nearly closed.

"Well?" demanded Anthony. "What does this mean?"

"The *iblis*, *sahib*."

"What of him?"

"I took four men and stalked him all through the night. He was dancing again. We came up with him and he ran. We followed. He ran very fast, skipping like a he-goat, but the moon favored us and we kept him in view.

"He came to bay at last in a *nullah*, and we called on him to surrender. He did not answer, but started to make magic to frighten us, waving with his arms thus—and thus. I gave the order to make him prisoner. So we left our rifles in charge of one man, and four of us rushed in to seize him."

"And didn't find it so easy, eh?"

"Nay, *sahib*, far from easy. He fought as I have never known a man to fight. He was stronger than a leopard. He struck with hands and feet—bit with his teeth—and all but tore the four of us limb from limb. And the man who held the rifles could not shoot because of the darkness and the risk of killing one of us. At last he had three of us senseless, but I broke loose from his hold and limped back for my rifle."

"Senseless, eh? Where are they now?"

"In hospital, general *sahib*. They were able to crawl home."

"You haven't told us where the iblis is," said Jim.

"Safe in *jehannum, sahib*."

"Dead, d'you mean?" asked Anthony. "How?"

"He died a natural death, general *sahib*."

"What—fell dead, d'you mean" Apoplexy—over-exertion or something?"

"Nay, *sahib*; my bayonet took him under the ribs and so upwards. He was a good fighter. The account is square between us."

"Where's the body? Did you leave it there?"

"Nay, general *sahib*. It says on the paper I should bring the prisoner in. We dragged it all the way between us, taking turns. The *dakitar sahib* says it weighs two hundred pounds."

"Dismissed, then. Go and get your wounds dressed," ordered Anthony.

www.ingramcontent.com/pod-product-compliance
Lightning Source LLC
Chambersburg PA
CBHW020143180626
46810CB00004B/1711